Christopher Caldwell
CALL AND RESPONSE
Neon Hemlock Press

NEON HEMLOCK

advance praise for
CALL AND RESPONSE

"Throughout, Caldwell brings his all-Black, mostly queer protagonists to vivid life while exploring the collision of the natural and the supernatural. This stuns."
—Publishers Weekly (starred review)

"*Call and Response* is a great showcase for Christopher's particular gift: his sophisticated prose, so changeable from story to story, but always distinctive in voice, playful and masterful in style!"
—Kai Ashante Wilson, author of *A Taste of Milk and Honey*

"I am so glad I get to live in the time-space where Christopher Caldwell is creating. And so happy to see these horny, heartbreaking, world-changing stories gathered together in one truly staggering collection."
—Sam J. Miller, author of *Boys, Beasts & Men*

"Christopher Caldwell's stories are lyrical and wondrous, his gaze unflinching and kind. Here are visions of doomed whaling voyages, bank robbers on the run from arcane enforcers, desperate characters confronting the world's evils, gods and saints, betrayals and joys. Caldwell calls us to witness the world as it is and as it could be. The tales in *Call and Response* are magic: they'll transform you."
—Izzy Wasserstein, author of *These Fragile Graces, This Fugitive Heart*

"*Call and Response* is one of the most honest, brutal and beautiful collections of short work I've ever read. It is full of love and pain and a will to not just endure, but thrive. Caldwell's rich characterization and voice infuses every story with a flesh and blood heart—a heart that will leap from the page and beat in time with your own. I am in awe of this collection. Thank you for writing it."
—Suzan Palumbo, author of *Skin Thief: Stories and Countess.*

Neon Hemlock Press
www.neonhemlock.com
@neonhemlock

© 2025 Christopher Caldwell

Call and Response: Stories of the Fantastic
Christopher Caldwell

All rights reserved. No part of this publication may be reproduced, stored in a retrieval system or transmitted in any form or by any means, electronic, mechanical, photocopying, recording or otherwise without the prior permission of the publisher or in accordance with the provisions of the Copyright, Designs and Patents Act 1988 or under the terms of any license permitting limited copying issued by the Copyright Licensing Agency.

This novella is entirely a work of fiction. Names, characters, places and incidents are the products of the author's imagination or are used fictitiously. Any resemblance to actual events, locales, organizations or persons, living or dead, is entirely coincidental.

Cover Design by dave ring
Interior Design and Layout by dave ring
Interior Illustrations by Matthew Spencer

Print ISBN-13: 978-1-966503-14-9
Ebook ISBN-13: 978-1-966503-15-6

Call and Response

• stories of the fantastic •

CHRISTOPHER CALDWELL

This collection of stories is dedicated to:

Sergio, because I promised so very long ago.
Mama, who was the first to call me to adventure.
November, who always responded, "Yes, good. Keep going."

i.

Call

ii.
Response

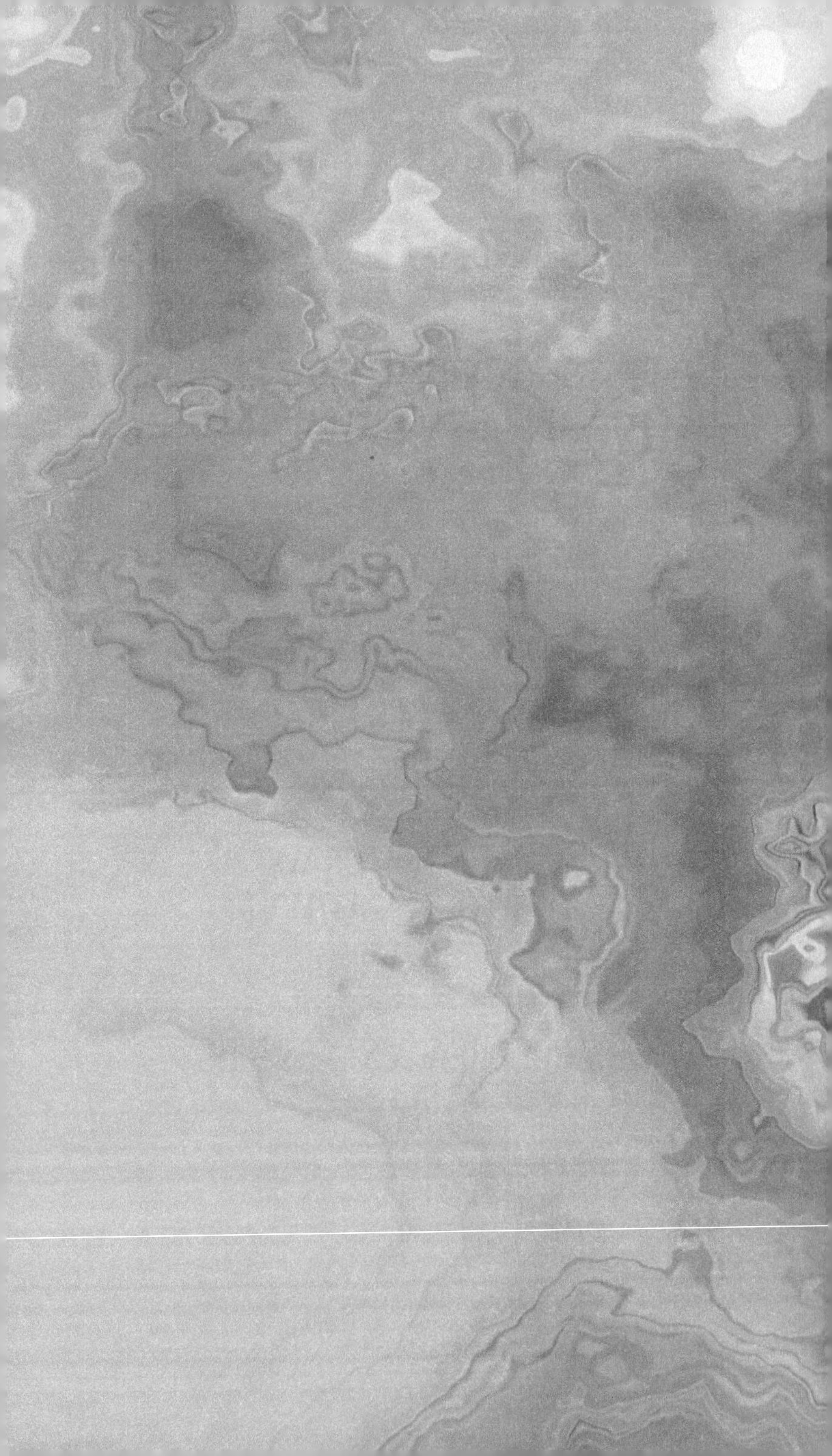

Call

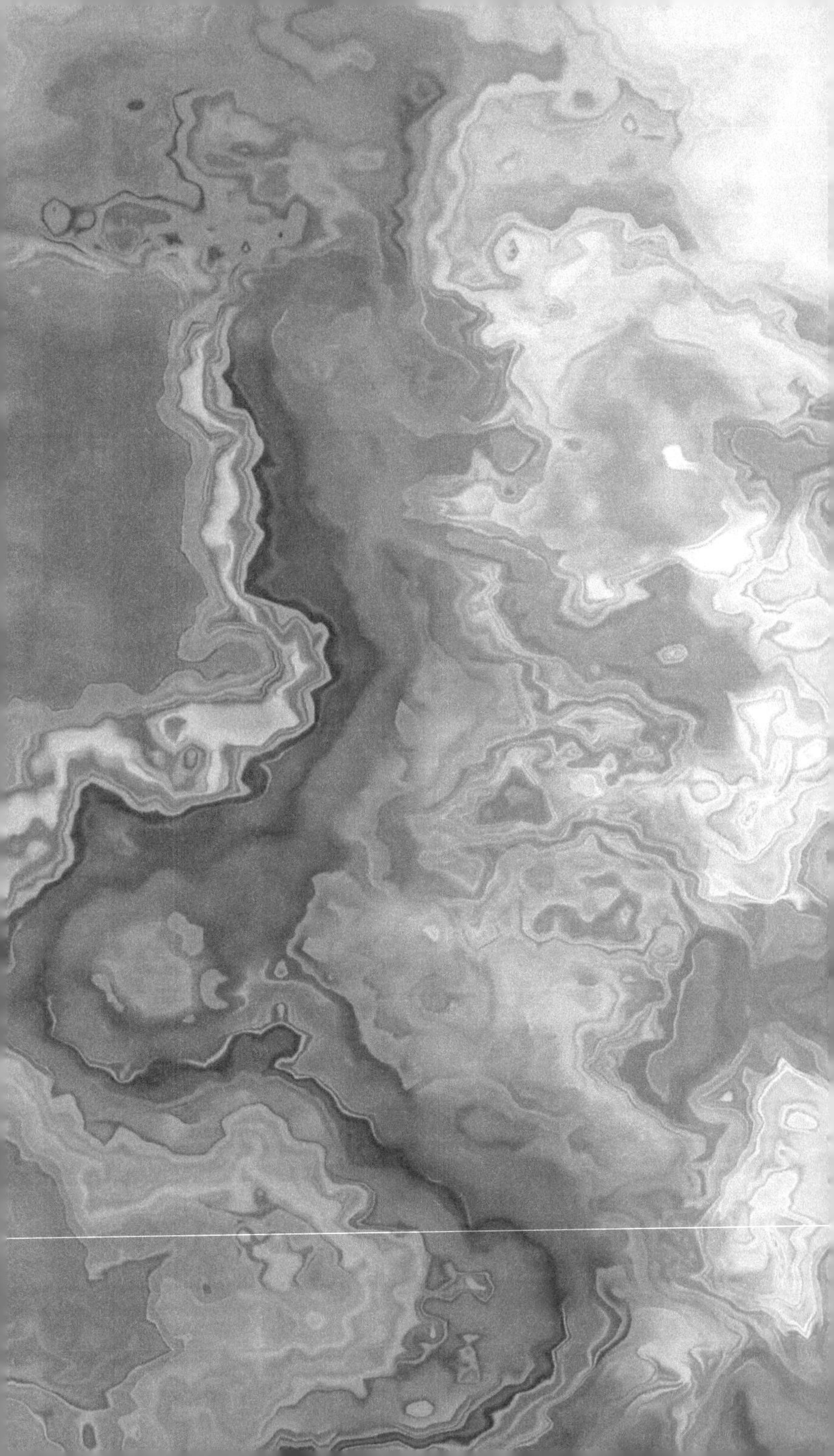

Femme and Sundance

I WAS 19 WHEN I met Tommy. A day and a bit into a two-day Greyhound trip from bumfuck, Nevada to Saint Paul, Minnesota. Going to meet some trick from the internet. Thought it was true love. Funky and itching for a smoke when we pulled into a truck stop in a one-road Nebraska town called Hendrickson or some shit. Big fat moon was high over the cornfields, and the diner gleamed all silvery. I was hungry, hadn't eaten nothing since a McDonald's outside Reno, so I finished my Newport and went in. You ever walk into a place where they hate everything you are? Them white folks stared at my fuchsia naps and mesh shirt like they couldn't decide if they were gonna call me "faggot" or "nigger."

I sat at the counter, gave the waitress my biggest "y'all sure fine people" grin and asked, "That good smell the meatloaf?"

She didn't smile back. "Meatloaf's the special today. We also got fried chicken if you like that better."

Ol' racist bitch. "I'll take me a meatloaf with extra gravy on the mashed potatoes, and a Coke. Where's the head?"

She pointed with her chin past the booths. "I'll get your order right in. Mind you don't miss that bus. Liable to leave without you."

What passed for a men's room was a dank closet with a toilet cubicle, one urinal and a sink someone'd pissed in. A naked lightbulb attracted moths overhead. I pissed in the urinal, worked fine, and easier access than the sink. Didn't wash my hands though. Looked myself over in the scratched-up mirror. My hair was flat on one side where I'd pressed my head against the bus window. I pulled a pick out of my back pocket. I'd locked the door, but it flew open with a bang. Big, blond, cornfed-looking motherfucker. About six feet tall, with freckles across his nose. Fuck. I'd left my Vaseline in my bag on the bus. If I was in for an ass-beating, I'd want something to keep his class ring from scarring up my pretty face. I clenched my fists and pushed my back to the wall. But the big boy's face got kinda soft and his lip trembled. He looked me up and down in a way I know damn well. "You're like some kind of angel from…"

I cut him off by kissing him hard. Whatever he saying was gonna be corny. Had to stand on my toes. He banged into the cubicle door. Fumbled with my belt. I pushed him down on his knees.

Half an hour later Tommy followed me onto that bus without even a change of clothes, his hair rumpled and shirt misbuttoned. We left that meatloaf congealing in its gravy right on the counter. I never did get to Saint Paul.

Most people look at Tommy think he's simple. He got them big blue eyes and that baby face and an aw shucks way of standing that makes you trust him. Looks like he ain't never had a devious thought in that head. But it was Tommy come up with the masks. He knew a curandera lived about an hour outside of Greeley, and to hear him talk, she had some tricks Sherlock Holmes couldn't never figure out. Tommy also had an Uncle Joe who was a mechanic and fixed up cars he got cheap at auctions. He sold us a Honda Civic for a song and an understanding that if we was up to no good we wasn't gonna say we bought it from him.

The bank was my idea. Big enough that we'd take in more than knocking off a couple of convenience stores, and far away from everything that we could get scarce before the law came down. We needed cash. Turning tricks in Wyoming won't fill anyone's pockets, and at 25, I was starting to get a little long in the tooth. Tommy's cigarette-ad-boy in a pick-up thing might last longer, but the prices he charged ain't never going back up. It don't cost much to rent a two-bedroom in the middle of nowhere, but when you can't count on pulling in nothing, not much gets expensive. I didn't always want my big Saturday night to be clean sheets at the Motel 6 and a bottle of Jim Beam.

So, one night after not much of nothing and rent coming up due, we decided we was getting out, and headed out towards Greeley, Colorado.

Big-ass sky overhead going down to Colorado. Always seems like purple clouds in the distance bristle with lightning. Pretty, but like driving through a picture. Motherfuckers get *restless*.

"How you know this bruja?" I asked, watching the light move like honey over some fucking amber waves of grain.

"Curandera."

"Whatever."

Tommy scratched at his chin. "Remember I told you about Spike Jimenez? Miz Boudreaux is his grandfather Hector's widow. His grandma died young, same as his ma. Hector and Miz Boudreaux practically raised Spike after his daddy went to state pen up in Lincoln?"

I grunted, and focused on the road. Tommy don't talk much, but when he gets going, he's like a dog with a bone, just jawing on and on.

"Anyway, one time in a game against the Sherman High Whirlwinds—they were our rivals, remember?—Spike gets sacked by this monster of a boy, musta been nearly three-hundred pounds, and just goes down with a crunch. They pull him off the field, but his arm is going into angles it shouldn't go, and just looks wrong. Miz Boudreaux pushes her way down from the stands, nobody stops her, she takes what looks like a dried frog from out her purse, puts it on Spike's arm and just kinda sings. You hear a snap like biting into a pretzel, and his arm is just fine. That's how I know. She's the real deal."

Wasn't nothing to argue with there.

We pulled up to the curandera's house at dusk. The clouds low against the far-off jagged line of the Rockies, like smoke escaping a ragged smile. Little ranch-style house. Yellow clapboard. Chain-link fence. Big neon blue and red fortune telling palm. The words Ms. Boudreaux's House of Healing painted by the door in red turned orange by the prairie sun. Tommy charged up the gravel front path, clambered up the porch, and then opened the screen door. He shouted in, "Miz Boudreaux?"

A voice from inside called out, "Thomas? Come in. Bring your friend. Sit down. I'll only be a moment."

We entered her living room. House smelled good. Like gumbo and lemon furniture polish. Old-people furniture covered with doilies. Paintings of saints, Martin Luther King, and angels. A miniature version of that famous statue of dead Jesus being held up by his mama was a cookie jar. It rested in the middle of the coffee table. Miz Boudreaux swept in through a beaded curtain across the doorway to the kitchen.

She looked like my auntie Josephine, a light-skin woman Uncle Jasper married a week after he met her in Houston. She said she was creole. Mama said she was a witch, and told me not to eat her spaghetti or anything red she made. Miz Boudreaux had that same coloring, the same high forehead, and the same sleepy, heavy-lidded eyes. Tommy popped off the virgin's head, and pulled out a crumbly almond cookie. Crunched.

Miz Boudreaux sat across from us. Rings glittered on her fingers. She pursed her lips. "Thomas! Your friend is very handsome."

"I'm Davion, ma'am."

She smiled at me. "Handsome and polite. Good. I worry that you end up with some no 'count trifling stoneheart. This soothes my heart."

I looked at my fingernails. Miz Boudreaux made a clucking sound. "No need to be shy." Her smile faded. She stared at Tommy pointedly for a second. "Now, this thing you want. We have already discussed my fee, but you must also both be aware of the costs."

I bit my lip. Ain't the first time I come across some extras raise the sticker price. Tommy furrowed his brow. "Now Miz Boudreaux, I promised you pretty much everything we got, honest."

She raised a hand. "I want no more of your money, Thomas. I can do things, yes? I can make charms that confuse the mind, I can enchant these things so electronics fail, I can do this. But it cannot come from nowhere!" The lights in the room flickered, long shadows danced across her face. "Your car, it need gasoline? My charms need fuel. The cost, my dears, is that for each minute you wear these masks, it will burn through a year of your life."

Tommy and me looked at each other. He grabbed my hand. Wasn't much of a life the way we were living.

"You must decide, both of you, how much life you want to give up. To make it work, I must bind that life into the charm. If you want this thing. If you do not, I understand."

I looked her in the eye. "Reckon fifteen minutes would do it."

Tommy nodded.

WHEN I SAY we dressed for the robbery, I want you to know we *dressed*. My jeans were Girbaud, my button-down Ralph Lauren, both our hats were Stetson, and we had on the nicest pairs of embroidered boots I could mop from the big leather outlet in Chickasaw. Tommy looked like a cowboy's dream in a red silk western shirt with fringe and roses. Ain't nobody going to remember what we wore or what we looked like thanks to the masks, but we knew, and I swear it made me walk a little taller, put a little swag in Tommy's chest.

We pulled into the parking lot of the bank on a Monday afternoon, just after the few shitty nightclubs in Jackson Hole had deposited their weekend takes, and before the ranchers down from the badlands came to take out cash to hide under the beds or whatever. Synchronized our ugly-ass digital watches. I opened the box with the masks. Tommy's had a long nose and crooked smile. It reminded me of the moon in that old McDonald's commercial. Mine was a sobbing face. Big blue, painted on tears on its cheek. We nodded. Set the watches. Counted to five. Put the masks on. It was like jumping into a cold pond on a hot day. My body shook and I felt my heart stop. A moment, then colors flashed gold and green and the world felt normal. I looked at Tommy through the eyeholes, but my vision kept sliding off of him, and when I tried to remember how he looked, all I could see was that damn McMoon. He said, "They work."

Right. Time was ticking. I grabbed the duffel bag. Out of the car and across the parking lot, duster flapping in the wind where no one could see it. Pistol in my hand, shotgun over Tommy's shoulder. Even if they couldn't focus on us, they'd know we meant business. Tommy kicked open the plate glass door. He trained his shotgun on the portly security guard who'd been chatting with a Miss Clairol redhead wearing an ugly string of fake pearls. There were screams. People hit the floor and hid under tables. I walked up to a teller, pistol aimed at her chest. A purse skittered across the room and landed at my feet. I kicked it away. I said loudly to the room, "We're planning on making a withdrawal. From the bank." I passed the duffel bag over to the teller. "No small bills, no marked notes, no little canisters that turn the money funky colors. Now, I'm not interested in your money, folks. Just the bank's, and all of that is insured. No one tries anything heroic, we all walk out of here nice and friendly." The tellers shoveled stacks of money into the duffel bag. I glanced at my watch. Three minutes, forty seconds gone. Stuffed near bursting, the teller shoved it back across the counter with some effort. I smiled, said, "Thank you, kindly."

Then there was a sound like thunder, and a smell like the fourth of July. Then I couldn't hear nothing but a high-pitched mosquito whine. I turned in the direction of the thunder crack. Tommy had blown a hole in the Clairol red, and much of the wall besides. She dropped to the ground. A dainty pink revolver spun away from her hands. Plastic pearls skittered across the floor. Tommy grabbed me by the wrist, and we both ran out the doors.

Masks off in the car at five minutes and forty-three seconds. Mouth tasted nasty, like I'd been sick. I started the engine, but couldn't hear nothing but that high-pitched whine. Tommy pulled out a pair of binoculars from the glove compartment and scanned behind us. I tried to put distance between us and the bank quick as I could without wrapping us around a telephone pole or ending up in a ditch. At some point, he switched on the radio, but the girls singing sounded like they fell into a tunnel, and I snapped it off.

Didn't stop driving until we reached the switch-off point about twenty minutes into Colorado. Ears rang the whole time. Didn't see the point of talking. When I closed my eyes, I saw fake pearls on ugly carpet spattered with blood. At the switch-off, we stripped. Girbauds, western shirt, gloves, boots, all into a pile in the back seat. Switched the money from the duffel bag into a couple of JanSports. Tommy splashed gas from a jerry can over the things, while I carried the JanSports to the cab Ford pick-up. He tossed a lit match. We sat in the flatbed of the truck bare-ass naked, pink doughnut box of masks between us, and watched the little Honda burn.

I turned to Tommy. "You think you shoulda maybe put that shotgun with them clothes?"

He shrugged. "It's a good gun."

"It's a murder weapon!"

"Well, I reckon it is." He spit on the ground.

ONCE WE GOT past Denver, Tommy stopped looking over his shoulder every six seconds. We passed the big green sign for the turn-off to Buffalo Bill's grave and I heard snoring. I drove through the Rockies in the dark with Tommy's rumbling for company, and felt less heavy each time we passed a turn-off or a junction. Time we got to the Eisenhower tunnel, I was almost back to my usual state of chill.

We stopped at a motel just outside the Siren city limits called the Lon-Tiki Inn. Big plastic Easter Island heads outside the office. Pool was drained and fenced off. Grey-faced old guy at the front desk handed us our key without any questions.

Room was mostly clean. Dusty red and orange carpet with a faded trail to the head. Palm trees on the wallpaper. King-size bed. Gideon's Bible on the nightstand. Wasn't neither of our idea of a tropical getaway, but I drove all night, and we weren't never gonna find a hotel with room service in Siren.

Tommy lugged the JanSports into the room. He picked up the purple one, unzipped it and covered the bed with cash. He pulled his shirt over his head and swung it around before flinging it onto a chair. Pulled his jeans and drawers down over his hips without unbuckling his belt. Kicked them off. Flopped down butt-naked in that pile of money. "Come here," he said. Then he plunked quarters into the slot for Magic Fingers machines atop the headboard.

You ever screwed on a pile of money with a bed bucking beneath you like a mechanical bull? I was still mad about the fuck-up at the bank, but wasn't like I could say no to that ass. Tommy's bigger than me, but I grabbed him by the hips and tossed him onto his stomach like he was some bird-boned twink. Bone-tiredness forgotten in my sudden need to fuck. No time for lube, I spit into my palm and slathered my dick. Tommy spread his thighs, desperate for it. The bed creaked and moaned beneath us, bumping up as we bumped together.

An hour later, we were sticky with cum and sweat, and plastered with Mr. Franklin's portrait in damp places. I was in need of a smoke. I peeled a $100 off my upper thigh, crumpled it and threw it in Tommy's face. "That shit did not go to plan."

He just laughed and twisted the cap off a bottle of Maker's Mark we picked up in Eagle. Took a swig. No chaser. "You think I was going to let some dried-up hero-playing bitch shoot you because of the plan? Baby, when I said I would kill for you—"

"I get it, Tommy." I stood up. Scratched my ass. "Don't think I ain't grateful. But in my head everything was so smooth. Now it ain't."

Tommy leaned back into the not-so-crisp money pile. Tried to make money angels. "Looks like smooth sailing to me, babe."

I scowled. "I need a shower. I smell like pits and ass." Put some of the money back in the JanSport. "It still spends. Jizz ain't the worst thing it's had on it."

I headed into the bathroom, grabbed a clean, threadbare towel. The back of my neck itched. There was an irritating sound like someone had the TV tuned to a dead channel with the volume all the way up. I figured I was just tired from the road. Hot water was soothing. I used one of those bullshit motel soaps and a washcloth to scrub the dirt off me. Turned off the shower. The itching and the sound was worse. I headed out to the main room. Tommy was sitting on the bed, jeans on, gun in his lap. He was facing the window. His shoulders looked tense. That sound got even louder. He half-turned towards me, mouthed "gun." My gun was sitting next to the TV, masks on either side of it. The masks, though, they were shaking. Like they was in tune with that stupid fucking static sound. I grabbed my gun, crouched down low behind the TV stand. Tommy rolled back down behind the bed. The itching spread down my spine, and up my jaw through my back teeth. I inhaled. The window shrieked. Glass cracked down like a lightning bolt. The door flew open, chain popping off. A smell like burning hair. Two figures entered. Black visors. Black padded jumpsuits covered with crazy silver stitches that twisted and glowed without any light. On their chests a triangular badge with the letters A, S, A at each corner. One was holding a thing that looked like a cross between a Geiger counter and a mute trombone, the other carried a big black box that made that sound. Box guy spoke. "We're only detecting six thaums. You might as well give it up. You'll die easier if you don't fight."

Tommy popped up from behind the bed. I heard three quick shots. Box guy fell back. Geiger counter turned his trombone on Tommy. I squeezed my trigger. One. Twice. Three times. Four. Hit him dead center. He fell back too.

I grew up with guns. My uncle taught me to shoot. Picked off coyotes that got too near his ranch. I ain't never shot a man before. My stomach turned. I tasted bile at the back of my throat. Doubled over, managed not to hurl. Tommy was cool, shrugged into his denim jacket. Grabbed the JanSports. Looked me in the eyes. "Davion, we got to go. Can you get the masks?"

I clutched both of the masks, still vibrating, to my chest and walked out into the early morning. Police sirens wailed in the distance. Tommy kicked the black box. The masks stopped vibrating. We put them on. Ran out to the pick-up past a fat man in a dirty wifebeater who stood at his motel room door, arms crossed. We piled into the pick-up and pulled onto the interstate, crossing over into Utah long before the Siren city police had time to figure out what had gone down at the Lon-Tiki.

SOME HOURS INTO Utah, after we traded the pick-up for a plum-red Chrysler from a shifty dealer outside of Green River who took too much money in exchange for a pointed lack of any sort of nosiness, we turned off into the back roads, and stopped for a picnic. We climbed a big, beautiful, dusty red rock almost as perfect as God made it, except for a small pile of whippits glittering near the edge. The rock seemed to drink in the sun's light, positively glowed. Tommy spread himself out on a blanket, took a bite out a sandwich and pointed at a cloud. "Looks like a really fat llama."

It did, and I laughed, and he laughed. The sound echoed out over the rocks. Black-winged birds with white throats scattered overhead. I took a bite of my cold, bullshit gas station cheese-and-bean burrito and a swig of warm Coke. My guts been clenched like a fist since Siren, and everything felt loose and light on that rock. I ate that trash burrito like it was my momma's banana pudding. I scooted close to Tommy on that ratty blanket and he wrapped his arms around me, and pressed his nose into the hollow at the top of my spine where my skull begins. The light was like honey.

"We fucked up. But everything's gonna be alright," I said. He nuzzled my neck. I rested my eyes for just a moment.

Tommy nudged me awake. "We better get off this rock afore it gets dark. I'm liable to break an ankle."

The day had turned orange and gold, and the sun was low. "Momma ain't raise no mountain goat," I said, and we packed up the blankets and the last bits of our rest-stop picnic. We scrambled down that rock with no more mishaps than a false step and a scuffed shoe.

I spotted a plume of dust kicked up by something and snatched up Tommy's binoculars. Off-road, in the distance I could see something a like a mail-truck but black, with a big version of the trombone thing from the Lon-Tiki on its top. "Fuck. Them assholes from Siren sent more a they busters after us."

"How'n the hell they find us again?" Tommy scowled.

The pink donut box rattled a little in the back seat. We looked at each other. "Masks," Tommy said.

I snatched them up out of the backseat. Made as if to fling the box into hell, but Tommy said, "Wait." He opened the box. The masks vibrated. "We leave these intact and we don't know if someone else could use 'em. We gotta bust them up."

Felt like a lump in my belly. I knew we wasn't coming back for them, but there was almost ten years left in each. Tommy picked up a big rock and brought it down on the masks. They *howled.* A coyote got into my uncle's rabbit hutch once, and the sound was like them rabbits, high, mean, and sharp. I felt a hitch in my chest, and the masks cracked when Tommy hit them again, then crumbled. He pitched the box away from him, put some spin on it. It tumbled down into a gulch.

We ran to the car and peeled out in the opposite direction. Tommy watched the black mail-truck thing through his binoculars. while I pushed that raggedy-ass Chrysler until it shuddered.

"They're following the box," he said. And I relaxed a little.

We switched the Chrysler out for a sky-blue Datsun, and after some detours and switchbacks, no more of that itchy feeling in the back of my head. We figured the trail had gone cold without the masks, but just in case I steered clear of Reno; too much of my own history tied up there. No plans and still with more money than two bodies ought to rightly have, we found ourselves heading towards California and the dream of canyon roads and beaches.

TOMMY AND ME stopped off at a hustler bar called Tuco's at a truckstop about a half-hour outside of Barstow along I-15. Had a neon peacock flashing his tail feathers on the sign outside. Windows blacked out for privacy.

On the inside: wood panelling, red pleather booths, velvet paintings of Crystal Gayle and Dolly Parton, a horseshoe hanging over the front door. Wasn't too busy when we got there at about two in the afternoon on a Tuesday. Two boys grinding on each other to a Deep House remix of Johnny Cash. Two others nursing beers on tap, one sucking the salt off roasted peanuts.

Tuco's was run by an old, mean queen named Sammy Ray who took over everything when his man, Big Tuco, got sick. Big Tuco got called that 'cause he looked like a meaty version of Eli Wallach in *The Good, the Bad, and the Ugly*. Sammy Ray wasn't no bigger than a poodle, and had a sweet, round face besides. But I've seen him deal with trouble in his bar with a baseball bat, and I know which of them I'd rather cross.

Sammy Ray ain't ask no questions about why we was flush, but we were buying rounds for the four sad-eyed boys waiting for the right kind of truckers to pull up, and he was pouring 'em stiff. I threw back a whiskey sour and wriggled on my bar stool to get a little closer to Tommy. We twined fingers. Sammy Ray reached up over the bar and clapped Tommy on the back. Rare bit of emotion behind Sammy Ray's steely eyes. "It sure is a good thing to see you two boys still together."

"Tommy's my ride-or-die," I said.

"We're like Bussy and Clyde," Tommy said. A little bit dizzy from whiskey sours and too many days on the road, we looked at each other and laughed until we gasped for breath. Tommy beat his chest and coughed. I wiped away tears.

"Femme Cassidy and the Sundance Kid!" I said. That set us off again.

Sammy Ray grinned. "I'm just glad you nasty boys didn't say something about *For a Fistful of Dollars*, because first of all—" He squinted his eyes and looked at the door. The horseshoe glowed a dull red, like a cast-iron skillet left on the burner too long.

A boom rattled the windows. Daylight flooded the room. Tommy shoved me off my stool. As I fell I saw a triangle of men in black padded uniforms storm in through the booted-open door. They opened fire. Tommy crumpled back against the bar. Drunk, on the floor, I wiggled to get my gun from under my shirt. Noise and smoke filled the room: screams from surprised twinks, breaking glass, and gunfire. The thundercrack of Sammy Ray's peacemaker.

One of those fuckers shouted, "They're not stunned!"

I turned towards the voice. I fired without aiming, into the light. My ears rang. I covered my mouth and coughed on the smoke and dust. Pulled myself upright, blinked. The horseshoe over the door cracked and fell to the ground in pieces. The twinks were crying. One of them was dead, slumped over in his booth. Spiderweb cracks laced the mirror behind the bar. Another twink clutched his stomach and howled. Tommy looked pale, one hand clamped his left shoulder, his shirt was red with blood. Sammy Ray stood over us, shotgun in his hand, his lips narrow and a vein bulging in his forehead. I moved over to Tommy, noticed a trickle of blood at his hips. Sammy Ray's voice sounded like it came from a bad long-distance connection. "What in the chicken-fucking hell did you dumb sumbitches do to pull a team of gotdamn arbiters to my bar?"

I tore a strip off my shirt and pressed it to Tommy's hip. My voice sounded like it came from an old floor-model TV. "What the fuck is an arbiter."

"Goddamn magic police. Called out for bad juju, not whatever chickenshit you two artless clowns was up to. Used up the interception charm on my horseshoe in one go. Only reason your dumbasses are still able to explain."

I pressed down on Tommy's wound. He gasped. Through gritted teeth, he said, "We might have pulled something using magical disguises. Don't know they found us." He winced. "We ditched them."

Sammy Ray's face softened. "You boys gotta get the fuck out of here. I can take care of this here mess, but they'll chase you anywhere in the States." He paused. "On the way out, check their trucks."

"Can you walk?" I asked Tommy.

He nodded. I helped pull him to his feet. He put an arm across my shoulders to steady himself. Outside was one of those black mail truck things we saw in the Utah desert. I peeked in the back. Our masks had been glued back together and stitched with silver thread and hooked up to wires on some sort of panel that looked like a submarine sonar from the movies. A radio crackled. A weird clock-looking thing with nine hands turned without any regard to the actual time. A pentagram was marked on the floor with LEDS at each juncture. Big silver pyramid on the wall with an eye like on the dollar bill with 'Arbitration Service of America' written in a circle around it. There were pictures of Miz Boudreaux and a map with glowing pins following our path from the bank. Tommy scowled. "What do we do?"

IT AIN'T HARD to find gasoline at a truckstop. Before those fuckers' backup showed up, we lit the masks up, and hell's mail truck along with it.

The Datsun died somewhere in Riverside county. Tommy's shoulder started to bleed again, and he was in no fit condition to walk to the next town, so we stood on the shoulder of I-15 with our thumbs out. Hours passed without much more than some curse words and half-empty big gulp thrown in our direction. The itching in the back of my teeth was back. Feeling cornered on the open road is not something I recommend.

Tommy turned to me, his big blue eyes wide and trusting. He coughed. "Maybe it's in my head. But do you feel that itching. Do you hear a sound like a cat scratch?"

I kissed him on the forehead. It was clammy. My heart thundered. "Naw baby. I don't feel nothing," I lied. "I think maybe you need to get some rest." I heard a squeal like the one before the windows rattled in Siren and sucked in my breath. A shadow loomed over us, and I prepared myself to go out fighting. But the squeal was the breaks of an eighteen-wheeler, and a big friendly-faced trucker in a plaid shirt leaned over to open his passenger door. "You boys looking for a lift?"

I gave my biggest smile. "Sure are, sir. Really appreciate it."

"Hop in." We clambered into the truck. Tommy leaned against me and shivered. He felt hot. The itching got stronger. I slammed the door shut.

"Where you boys headed?"

"To Mexico, sir. But as far as you can take us would be grand."

He laughed. "Wish I was young enough to enjoy Mexico like I bet you fellas will. I'm going to San Diego, but I figure that's close enough for you boys to find your own way south."

I pulled out a wad of cash from one of the JanSports, desperate to put some distance between us and the itching.

The driver shook his head. "I didn't pick you boys up with any expectations. Keep your money, just do someone else a good turn."

Tommy moaned softly. He needed a doctor, but it wouldn't do him no good if we couldn't get away from them arbiters. They had to be close. The driver pulled back onto the highway. I kept my eyes on the road and tried to ignore the bad taste in the back of my mouth. Fifteen years gone. What if Tommy was only meant to live fifteen more years? Shania Twain was on the radio, but the itching drove out the bubblegum brightness of her song.

Tommy looked bad, and the driver sang along, and all I could think was to pray that nothing happened to this kind man as I looked in the rearview mirror. But nothing looked like a black mail truck, and slowly the itching subsided.

So, Mexico. It's been almost two years since we crossed the border. We settled on a little town in Baja. Tommy's learning to fish and I'm learning Spanish. It's slow, and folk mostly laugh at my pronunciation, but I can understand what's being said to me. Tommy don't hardly speak English no more, them Spanish words slide off his tongue without a pause in-between them. He ain't never recovered the full use of his left hand, and he walks with a limp, but he plays fútbol with the muchachos on Sunday and can pound out masa into a passable tortilla. JanSport money ain't going to last us forever. But I got me a job at the carnicería cutting up hogs, and we make do. We watch the sun go down over the ocean together most nights. In the spring, sometimes you catch sight of a whale.

We ain't never tired of each other's company. We both know our time together is going to be shorter, but damn if that don't make the silliest things have meaning. Each time Tommy tells a bad joke or tickles my neck is a blessing. And if sometimes we jump at an itch at the back of our necks, or my stomach drops because a stranger stands in a shaded alley wearing all black, well that don't seem too high a price to pay.

The Lonesome Sea

THE FOG FROM the Chesapeake turned the morning light thin, like watery grits. The rainbow-ringed moon still hung low in the east, when Phillippian, full of business, roiled into the cookhouse, sopping wet, bare-chested, arms full of oysters. Brackish water cascading from his body and soaked trousers splattered onto the hard packed earth floor. Miss Sarah was kneading dough for bread. She wiped her hands on her apron and gave the boy a perfunctory cuff on the back of the head. "You make more work for me before I break my fast, and I'll dine on a slice of your backside, meager as it is."

Chastened, the boy carefully spilled his bounty onto a long, low table. "Caught you fat oysters fresh from the bay at first light, Miss Sarah. Reckoned you could sample a few long before marse Josiah makes his way down to the table."

The cook shoved a heavy Dutch oven onto the fire and moved to appraise Philippian's haul. She plucked an oyster from the pile and held it in one scarred, battered hand, while pulling a short knife from the waist of her apron with another. Shucked, the meat inside was tender, and plump. She gave the boy a rare smile. "Well done, although if the master discovers you have been diving, he's liable to send you under the *Sweet Ceres* to scrape the barnacles from her hull and save him time in drydock."

Phillippian helped to shuck the oysters, separating out the ones to be smoked from the ones for the stewpot by size. "Corinthian said Big Jim bought his freedom from Marse Thomas Davis. You reckon if I find a pearl in one of these oysters Marse Josiah would let me buy mine? I'm only small."

"Your sister chatters too much and works too little. Master Josiah is not best pleased with her needlework on the sails." Sarah sighed and placed a fist at the small of her back. "Besides, these aren't oysters that pearls come out of."

"But with La Sirène all things are possible, Miss Sarah." Phillippian's eyes were wide and earnest.

"You tell no lies." She ruffled the boy's kinky hair with surprising tenderness. "Now quick, before Master Josiah gets up and tells me to hot up the last of yesterday's stringy old hen, show me you've been practicing your letters."

AT MIDDAY, AFTER Master Josiah had Caleb drive him into town in the phaeton pulled by borrowed horses, Corinthian rushed past Phillippian, who was carrying logs for the fire into the cookhouse. Her eyes were wild. An unruly plait stuck out of her cap.

Miss Sarah turned to her. "Co-rinthian Gal, by what purpose are you here in the cookhouse, and not engaged in the quiet industry of sewing sails?"

"Miss Sarah, ma'am." She drew herself to her full height, half a head taller than Phillippian, but eye level with Miss Sarah's bosom. "The blockade, ma'am. It's all the talk. They say Adam Armstrong loaded his Morning Revalee with cotton duck, and tried to run the blockade in darkness, but the British were wise to it, and seized her off the coast, cotton duck and all!"

Miss Sarah scowled. "Master Armstrong's misfortune is not your gain. Attend to your hair, you look a state!"

Corinthian shook her head. "That's not all! They say they impressed all the white men into the navy to help fight old Boney, but they offered the negroes their freedom if they would serve in the colonial marines!"

Phillippian whispered that word, *freedom*, letting it roll around in his mouth. He stood on his toes and helped Corinthian tuck her hair back into her cap.

Miss Sarah stirred the stew in its cauldron. It was fragrant with onions that had just begun to turn. "Master Josiah's ship is in dock, and it's a poor merchant whose goods can't pass beyond the harbor. You're of an age to start whelping pick-a-ninnies, so you best pray trade resumes before Master Josiah notices and is off to market with you, narrow hips and all."

AT DAY'S END, Phillippian and Corinthian scrubbed the oyster shells clean, buffing the nacre until it shone. Miss Sarah poured a little rum into a tin cup. Corinthian took four of the smoked oysters and laid them on a piece of bread glistening with bacon fat. Phillippian carried the oyster shells and a string of wooden beads. The three of them walked down to the shore in procession bearing their gifts. lantern lights in the distance reflected off the water.

They laid the gifts on an altar of smooth, cool stone. The tide was coming in, and brackish water lapped against Phillippian's ankles as he arranged the shells.

"Thursday belongs to Agwé," Miss Sarah said. "It is right that we thank him and La Sirène for their gifts."

Corinthian shook a little rattle made from shells and driftwood, and hummed low as Miss Sarah said words of praise.

"We thank you, Agwé, for keeping our bellies full and hearts light. We thank La Sirène for her care."

Corinthian nudged Phillippian and shook the rattle.

Phillippian's voice was small. "Agwé, sir? They say there's no cooking deep in the sea, so we cooked you a meal, with rum to warm you and your bride."

Miss Sarah turned her back to the bay and spread her arms wide, as if to embrace both children. "Many years from now, when your life is at an end, it is Agwé who will sail you across the lonesome sea home at last to Guinee on his ship, *Immamou*."

A sudden wave crashed into the little altar, knocking over the tin cup of rum. The rum pooled on the sand before vanishing.

JOSIAH ATWOOD WAS pinch-faced with a slightly derelict air. In prosperous times his clothing ran towards well-darned; at present his breeches were threadbare. Fingers on his right hand purpled with ink. He carried a large ledger under one arm. He came across Phillippian hauling up water for Miss Sarah.

"Boy," he said. He never used Phillipian's name as though he had a vast retinue beyond counting, although in truth he employed four slaves. "You're a strapping lad of nine or ten summers," —Phillippian was eight and small for his age— "and Caleb tells me you're clever, besides. I have a mind to take you as a cabin boy. You may be wasted in the scullery."

The boy looked at the ground. "Yes, marse Josiah, sir."

Josiah pursed his lips and walked around Phillippian in a slow circle. "Tell me boy, what do you know? What can you do?"

Phillippian opened his mouth, then remembered Miss Sarah warning that he must never let a white man know he knew his letters, and his teeth crashed together.

Josiah coughed. "I heard you speak. You're not dumb, boy."

Phillippian squeaked. "No, Marse! Sir! I can swim, and chop firewood, and hold my breath underwater, and clean a hen, and peel potatoes, sir!"

"Can you climb a rope, boy?"

"Yes, marse! Quick as anything!" Phillippian tried to stand a little taller.

"Good, good. Tell me, do you suffer from poor digestion? Are you prone to seasickness?" Josiah gripped his chin with his ink-splattered hand.

"No marse Josiah, Miss Sarah says I eat healthy like." Phillippian furrowed his brow. "I can't rightly say about seasickness. But I've been knocked about by waves, and it's not done me harm."

"Wager you'll take to knots. We'll teach you to hand, reef, steer, yet." Josiah gave Phillippian an appraising look. "You're for my cabin boy on the *Sweet Ceres*."

PHILLIPPIAN RUSHED INTO the cookhouse with two buckets of water, slopping a little on the ground in his haste. Miss Sarah was plaiting Corinthian's hair. She looked up as he came in. "Is your intent to convince me that you have moved with all speed, instead of hauling my water at a gentleman's leisurely pace?"

"Ow!" Corinthian said as Miss Sarah untangled her hair with a comb.

"Hold still, gal! I know you're tender-headed, but squirming makes it worse." Miss Sarah's gaze was firmly on Phillippian.

"I wasn't at play, ma'am! I went straight to the well, and there I encountered marse Josiah!" Phillippian beamed with delight. "He wants to take me, *me,* as his cabin boy aboard the *Sweet Ceres*!

Corinthian squealed, this time with joy. "Imagine our Phillippian on the high seas! Cutting a dashing figure, brave as anything!"

Miss Sarah furrowed her brow. "Not my place to say, but I would think you're young yet for even a cabin boy at the best of times. And with all this blockade business!" She sighed and looked resigned. "Come sit by my feet whilst I braid your sister's hair. I'll teach you a reel for sailors to sing to Agwé while you're out there on his sea."

Corinthian clapped her hands. "If you get taken by pirates, and they make you as cruel and deadly as Black Caesar himself, remember us here on the land kindly!"

Miss Sarah sucked her teeth. "Black Caesar been dead near a hundred years. It's the British Navy that's Phillippian's concern."

THE *SWEET CERES* was a two-masted schooner that in prosperous times was crewed by sixteen men. But she set sail in the dead of night with a crew of eleven grown men and one small boy. Master Josiah himself piloted her. The crew boarded one by one, in silence. Phillippian followed the boatswain, Adam Carter, a wiry man with thinning hair, watery blue eyes, and skin tanned brown as new saddle leather. The boatswain held a dark lantern as a

source of light, and with furtive hand gestures indicated
to the crew their tasks as the boat slipped out from the
docks. Abel Rowe, who had done three years on a whaler,
clambered up the rigging to keep watch on the horizon for
ships from the Royal Navy.

The waters were a vast blackness before Phillippian,
while the city was pinpoints of light behind. He craned
his neck trying to make out Miss Sarah's cookhouse,
but before he could be sure of its location, a gruff voice
called out, "Pip!" The boatswain had determined that
Phillippian was too much of a mouthful. "Eyes on me, I'll
learn you how to trim a sail."

"Aye, Bo's'n," Phillippian said.

In the starless dark, with only the dark lantern's faint
light, the boy and boatswain set about catching the wind.

DAWN FOUND THEM on the high seas with no sight of the
Royal Navy giving chase. In celebration, Philllippian
had been given half a portion of watered grog, which he
poured over the side in silent offering to Agwé. He was
unsteady and unused to the waves' undulation, but there
was no time for rest. As cabin boy, he was called to attend
to Master Josiah's toilet, and serve his breakfast afterward.

Josiah wrote in a heavy, leather-bound ledger while
picking at cold chicken and hard cheese with his free hand.
He wrote in a jerky, untidy manner, in sharper letters than the
elegant, flowing hand Phillippian learned from Miss Sarah.
Drops of ink splattered from his quill, blotting the page. It was
still legible to Phillippian, who stood behind Josiah holding
a cloth for the man to wipe his hand clean of chicken
grease, although some words were strange to him, such as
disengaged. It seemed to be an account of their passage out
from harbor, with some small embellishments added.

Josiah stopped scratching with his quill and turned to Phillippian who had the sense to look away, as if uninterested in the scrawled word. Josiah coughed. "Cold chicken and crumbly cheese will seem a luxury when we are reduced to dining on salt pork and hard tack, and the wine has gone sour, my boy."

Phillippian, who had broken his fast on cornmeal mush, said nothing.

Josiah clapped him on the back. "Come boy, there's a full day's sailing awaiting us. The Bo's'n's keen on inspecting your knots."

Phillippian followed out onto the deck, attempting to mimic the rolling gait the crew adopted.

THE FIFTH NIGHT out, steady on his sea legs, hands sore from rope burn, stinking of sweat and sea water, Phillippian fell into his hammock. A wind from the southwest had turned the sea rough, but sleep found him quickly nonetheless.

In dreams, he found himself submerged in a vast sunken hall lit throughout by innumerable jellyfish, each smaller than a child's hand, but radiating a cold, blue light. Columns of coral and sea-smoothed glass stretched far above him into darkness. He knew without being told that he was far beneath the ocean, but felt suffused with calm and peace, rather than panic. Jewel-bright anemones wriggled luminescent tendrils independent of the currents; sun colored fish darted between them. At the far end of the hall, a gossamer veil parted and revealed a pearl as big as an oxcart. Enthroned on the pearl sat a hooded figure in white. Phillippian found himself kneeling on the sandy floor below the figure. There was a hand mirror in the figure's lap, framed with silver and seed pearls. The figure raised a hand and drew back his hood. Phillippian looked up into the face of a handsome young man, with brown, smooth skin, long eyelashes, and wild curls that floated upwards. His eyes were a startling green, like the bay in high summer.

"They call you Phillippian, like Paul's letters to the Romans, is that so?" The man's voice was a rich baritone, with a timbre that belied his apparent youth. "Do you know me, Phillippian?"

The boy trembled but held the man's gaze. "I know you, my lord Agwé, prince of the deeps, captain of *Immamou*."

Agwé cupped Phillippian's face with a long-fingered hand. "You have offered me many gifts and devotions and find yourself now passing through my demesnes. As your host, I offer a gift in return."

Agwé held out the mirror in his lap, which became a handsome little awl embellished with mother-of-pearl accents on the handle. Phillippian took it, felt the comforting weight of it. He bowed his head, and began to offer thanks, when the hall and all in it dissolved into darkness. He was rocked awake by a rough jolt of the waves and found himself in his little hammock.

But when he got his bearings, he found the little awl still clutched in his right hand.

A FORTNIGHT OUT. Phillippian had taken a hand to everything. He learned to read directions in the stars, to tie all manner of knots, to mend sails, to catch fish startled in their shoals by dolphins. When Abel Rowe fell from the rigging during a squall, Phillippian learned how to make a splint and set a broken bone from the ship's carpenter, Old Ben.

Josiah left the helm to take lunch and invited the boatswain to join them. Phillippian served them both soup and hardtack and poured glasses of wine from the captain's private store. He stood at attention. But Josiah dismissed him with a wave. "No need for you to wait on us, boy. You can be of use elsewhere."

"Aye, Captain." Pip bowed and left the two men, who leaned over the table conspiratorially.

Phillippian was on deck splicing damaged lines when a trick of the wind carried voices over to him. The boatswain's voice was low. "You're the cap'n, aye, and you know your business well enough, but you'd be a fool to sell wee Pip on. Boy takes to the sea like he was born to it."

"There's a little of the wine left, Mister Carter." Josiah sounded annoyed. "I'll have the boy bring up another cask tomorrow. I gave you permission to speak plain, and I appreciate your candor. I have debts to consider, and as much as we are making good time to France, I fear that this venture will only just be profitable."

A grunt. "Aye, Cap'n. But I reckon you can keep the better part of the boy's lay." Both men laughed at this.

PHILLIPPIAN COUNTED TWENTY-SEVEN days before they sighted land. On the twenty-eighth, they sailed into an old stone harbor. It was a chilly day, and the waters seemed gray and dark to Phillippian's eyes. The crew grew frantic with excitement. Abel Rowe boasted about his prowess with French harlots, while Old Ben warned younger sailors not to spend their entire lay on sour cider. Phillippian attended to Josiah's toilet and shaved him. Josiah had the boy air his velvets and silks from their trunk, and managed to cut a respectable figure, if a little dated in fashion to the continental eye.

Before anyone could take shore leave, bolts of cotton duck and bales of tobacco needed to be taken up from the hold, accounted for, and bundled for sale and transport. It was hard, heavy work, and Phillippian assisted as best he could, but his size worked against him.

Phillippian was selected to stay on the ship, with a sallow, quiet sailor known only as Quinn, who was only vocal about his displeasure at the men's whoring and carousing. From the deck, Phillippian marveled at the hand-painted signs adorning the low, clustered buildings along the waterfront, written in letters he could make out, but words that were meaningless to him. Quinn said, "A godless place. They'd turn you into a filthy heathen, make no mistake. Best not to subject yourself to wickedness."

Phillippian was wistful. "Only Miss Sarah said they made lace fine as spider's webs in France, and I'd like to get Corinthian a ribbon to tie up her hair. It flies out of her cap something awful."

Quinn muttered, "Who can find a virtuous woman? For her price is far above rubies." His look was sour and dismissive.

LONG AFTER DARK, the sailors began returning to the ship. Some singing loudly, some weeping. Phillippian heard Abel Rowe brag to Samuel Brand: "There were four of them! And me with only one good arm! I said, 'mademoiselle, you'll have to be careful of me splint!'"

Josiah and the boatswain boarded together. Josiah's cheeks were flushed and his gait light. It appeared his negotiations had gone well. The boatswain's gaze was stony.

Josiah tossed the boy a small silver coin. "Here, have this as a souvenir, my lad! French! With the Emperor's own image on it!"

Phillippian secreted the coin away in his shirt next to his trusted awl.

Quinn whispered to him later, "Not half a yard of the most moth-eaten lace would that coin buy you. Wear not your gratitude too dearly."

THEY SET SAIL early the following morning. Sailors whose heads were split from too much drink swearing and cursing the dawn. Live ducks, cured hams, and ropes of dried sausage made their return provisions seem more enticing than the last week's rations of cornmeal mush and salt pork.

The boatswain clapped Phillippian on the shoulder. "Captain dined at the home of the mayor himself. A French mayor! Reckon he'll have airs and graces at the table now, and want the finest cookery."

Phillippian nodded. "But no one puts on a finer table than Miss Sarah, and we're homeward bound, Bo's'n."

The grin faded from Mister Carter's face. "Homeward bound, aye. Help me work this line."

There was no need to depart in silence this time, and Old Ben sung out in a deep, strong voice as they pulled up the anchor. "Oh, there was a lofty ship, and she set out to sea! And the name of the ship was Golden Vanity! And she sailed 'pon the low and lonesome low."

Other sailors joined in, even Quinn, his voice cracking a little, "And she sailed upon the lonesome sea!"

THE WINDS WERE in their favor. There was still more than enough work to go around, and Phillippian found himself using his little awl to help repair sails late into the evening after spending the day waiting on Josiah, helping Old Ben with small repairs, and shouting "Aye Bo's'n!" in response to the frequently bellowed "Pip!" But Josiah's temper was sweeter, and he seemed less frantic when scrawling down notes in his ledger. Abel Rowe, who was still some ways off from climbing the rigging, taught Phillippian how to identify sailing ships by ensign and jack from a distance, and how to call out bearing.

Phillippian kept count of the days, and when he marked a Thursday, he found some time to himself in the evening to make an offering to Agwé and sing to him and La Sirène just as Miss Sarah had taught him.

On a night where the black heavens spilled over with stars, the full moon rose above the dark seas, as lustrous as the pearl-throne in Phillippian's dream, casting a road of light across the waves. He was sure it was meant to guide him home.

A FORTNIGHT AND six days on the return, Phillippian awoke in darkness. The man-stink of the sailors and their snores and somnolent eructations were now familiar and comforting to the boy. He climbed down from his hammock and stood barefoot on the deck. As he waited very still in the dark, he heard a low rumbling from beneath him. His heart fluttered in his chest. The rumbling became a voice, a dread voice loud as the storm. "Phillippian?"

The boy looked around, but the half-seen forms of sleeping sailors did not stir. He whispered, "Yes?"

The voice was the roar of the ocean. "Read his ledger."

The rumbling rattled the small boy's frame, then ceased. He fell to his knees trembling. When he put his hand to his awl, the metal was warm.

DAWN FOUND PHILLIPPIAN attending to Josiah for his morning toilet. The boy was solicitous and soft-spoken as he shaved his master, his eye on the ledger.

"Marse Josiah, will you take your breakfast in the cabin this morn?"

The man snorted, sitting very still as Phillippian slid the razor across the soft flesh beneath his chin. "No, boy. Mister Carter and I need to make preparations for evading the Royal Navy. Not long until they're a problem again, I fear."

Phillippian rinsed the blade of lather. "Aye marse Josiah. Shall I air your cabin and freshen your night linens, sir?"

Josiah squinted. The cabin had taken on an appreciable musk. "Yes, that's good, boy. Abel can tell you what to look out for, I'd wager." He regarded himself in a beaten brass hand mirror. "Good close shave, boy."

Phillippian found himself alone in the cabin. After a few moments of making pretense of cleaning, he made for the red leatherbound ledger sitting on the captain's table. It was locked. Phillippian swore softly and pulled out his awl. No sooner than it touched the keyhole did the clasp spring open. He gasped in surprise. He opened the book. Josiah had marked the most recent entry with a ribbon. Phillippian worked backwards, skimming over columns of numbers that were meaningless to him. An entry from not long after the *Sweet Ceres* set sail from France read: "The repast at M. Guillemet's home remains memorable. Will have to invest some of the profits in buying a girl equal to her quality as a cook." Phillippian frowned. Miss Sarah was an excellent cook.

Phillippian eyed the door warily, then turned back to the ledger. He scanned through complaints about Abel Rowe's injuries and his perceived uselessness, and uncharitable assessments of the boatswain's intelligence. At long last he came across an entry early on the voyage, written in a cramped and furtive hand. "All of my negroes sold, excepting the boy who was too small to garner a good price. The cook is a loss, and one not easily replaced, but there is no need now to maintain a kitchen. The girl sold well, doubtless due to her coming from a brood of seven, and her potential uses as a good breeder."

Philllippian clasped a hand over his mouth to strangle a scream. He read the passage again, holding the ledger open with trembling hands. All of my negroes. Excepting the boy. Caleb gone! Miss Sarah, near as Phillippian had to a mother, sold off like a bale of tobacco. Corinthian, his sister, his own blood, his last remaining link to family, given over to be a brood mare. Phillippian clenched his fists. He bit down on his lip, drawing blood, unaware of it until the hot salt taste of it. Josiah's razor lay on a cloth across from him, and for a wild moment Phillippian saw himself take up the razor, saw himself slashing it across marse Josiah's lying throat like a spring pig. A frisson of pleasure surged through him as he imagined the man's hot blood pooling on the cabin floor. But he closed the ledger, and pushed the clasp lock back into place. He put his hand on the smooth handle of his awl, and then remembered the little coin. He pulled it out from its hiding place in his shirt and threw it to the floor in disgust.

PHILLIPPIAN WAS WITHDRAWN and sullen in the days that followed. Josiah took no notice. His shave remained close, and his meals served promptly and courteously. If there was a drop more moisture in the wine or in the stew from the spittle of a small boy, it was not apparent to him. The boy anticipated his master's needs, and Josiah had no great like of chatter.

It was Mister Carter who saw the boy's sour mood plainly and broached the subject. "Pip, lad. Your eyes have lost their shine. You don't join in with Old Ben's songs. Summat weighing your heart down?"

Phillippian took to lying much easier than he had imagined. "Aye, Bo's'n. It's only that we must make landfall soon, and that means skirting the blockade. They say the Royal Navy is cruel and I fear them."

Mister Carter untied the brass spyglass he wore at the hip and proffered it to Phillippian. "You'll be on lookout duty for Abel Rowe, I wager. You keep us right."

"Aye, Bo's'n," he said with a false smile.

THREE DAYS LATER, just before nautical twilight, Phillippian was aloft in the crow's nest, and he caught sight of the black hulk of a sailing vessel in the distance. In the fading light, he could just make out the jack of the British Navy. He shouted the alarm and called out its bearing, before descending to the deck below.

Josiah clutched his sextant with a death grip. He was arguing with the boatswain. "Surrender? To have all my goods stolen, and my crew impressed? Even should I be allowed to return home, there would be nothing left to me but ruin and calumny!"

"Aye, Cap'n, but she'll have a full crew and there's little chance we might outrun her, and her less that we outgun her."

Abel Rowe moaned. "I'm not for going back to Bristol!"

Quinn mumbled a quick prayer while gazing balefully in the direction that Phillippian called out. Old Ben wept openly.

Phillippian spoke in a small, calm voice. "Marse Josiah? Cap'n? What will you give me if I sink the British ship before she takes us?"

The crew laughed. But Josiah's look was appraising and desperate. He stroked his chin. "What do you ask?"

A slow, cruel smile spread across the boy's face. "If I can sink that ship, I'd ask for freedom, for myself, for my sister, Corinthian, and for your cook, Miss Sarah. And I'd ask for my lay, of course."

Mister Carter stared at the boy. "How's a bit of a lad like you reckon to sink a man of war?"

Phillippian shrugged. "If I sighted them, then they have as like sighted us. I'm a good swimmer, and strong. I can hold my breath for a long time. When they close the distance in the dark, I'll dive into the ocean, and punch holes in her from below. They'll take on water, with no time to repair."

Old Ben opened his mouth in protest. But Josiah's eyes had a sly gleam. The captain said, "Aye boy. All that and more if you sink her. All that and more."

Mister Carter said, "Boy, this is foolishness."

But darkness had come, and it was a night with no moon. Phillippian stripped to the waist, gripped his awl in his right hand and dove over the side, plunging into the water below.

The waters were cold, and dark. Phillippian surfaced for a moment to take in a deep breath of air. He could see the British ship moving close, lanterns ablaze. He dove down. The awl glowed with a soft blue light. Beneath the waves, he could see the hulls of the *Sweet Ceres* and the swiftly approaching British ship. His chest tight, heart hammering, he swam towards one, the awl lighting his way. It found its mark, and he punched up. It sliced through the wood as if it were butter instead of oak, making a hole bigger than Phillippian's fist. He punched up with the awl twice, three times, swam further, and six, seven, eight times. He could hear the distorted groaning and cracking of the wood, as the water rushed in from below. Ten, eleven, twelve. His lungs pounded for air, but he continued his work, until at last the ship began to drop down. He swam from beneath the hull as quickly as he could manage, found a clear space in the water and surfaced, gasping from breath.

He heard screams of panic and shouts from the *Sweet Ceres*, then a terrible cracking roar as her beams split and the second of her two masts sheered off. Then she was swallowed into the sea, which takes all things, and the world was silent. Phillippian made a sad little gasp, but then found himself sucked under as the ship passed below.

He struggled against the pull of the depths, using the light of the awl to guide him. He twisted away from flotsam that rose past him. He found himself caught in rigging like a fish, and struggled to free himself but in that struggle lost grip of the awl, which tumbled down end over end below him. In the cold and dark he found a piece of wood, smooth and carved with the figure of a woman. The goddess Ceres, the lost schooner's figurehead. He clung to this, wrapping his arms around its waist, weeping as they fell. Presently, the downward motion stopped, and the boy and figure were buoyed up as if by some unseen force. They broke the surface, and the boy gasped for breath. Then vomited seawater as he clung to the figurehead.

He saw lights on the water, and a ship moved towards him in the darkness. Dizzy and half-dead, he thought it must be at last the *Immamou*, come to take him home to Guinee.

An English voice cried out, "Ahoy there!"

Phillippian weakly cried back, "Ahoy!"

It was a matter of minutes before they had him aboard and wrapped in blankets. Shivering and safe, he looked out over the night-dark expanse of the ocean and thought of the bright sunken hall and its gentle prince that rested far beneath. A long-nosed man with a worried air asked his name. He answered, "They call me Pip."

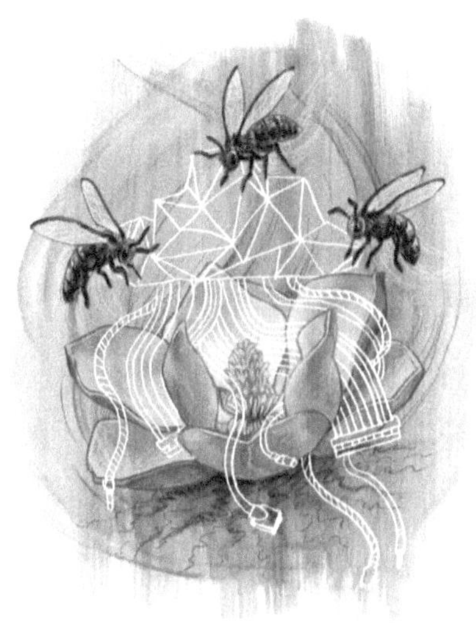

The Beekeeper's Garden

OVERWHELMED BY THE intermingled scents of jasmine, wisteria, and gardenia, the girl slammed shut the sash window in her tiny room. The lace-trimmed curtains still reeked of the four-o-clocks that bloomed in the window box the evening before. From the kitchen she could hear the woman—she would NOT think of her as Mother Bea—humming her song as the kettle whistled. The girl knew after the woman had her tea, made weak with milk and sweetened with honey, she would take out the straightening comb and place it on a burner until it glowed a dull red. Counting on having maybe four minutes to herself, the girl pushed her little bed away from the wall, steadying the brass headboard with one hand so that its creak would not give her away. On hands and knees in the little space behind the bed, she pulled back a strip of floral wallpaper near the baseboard. Along the bottom of the bare wall were the names: Dear, Auntie Denise, Mama, and Big Nanny written in a childish scrawl in rust-brown letters. She bit down hard on her thumb, wincing a little, but not daring as much as a gasp. Blood beaded in the ball of her thumb, and she added the name Gramma Augusta to her list. The humming from the kitchen stopped. She replaced the strip of wallpaper—it darkened slightly where it touched the fresh blood—then she pushed the bed back into place. The girl heard the teacup clatter in the sink. The click click click of the gas burner. The *fwoomp* of its flame. She smoothed down the front of her dress, hoping that she had swept beneath her bed well to keep her stockings white. There were no mirrors in the house. Right on schedule, the woman's voice rang out from the kitchen: "Come and let Mother Bea comb that tangled hair, Sarah sweetheart."

Not my name, the girl thought. She clenched her fists, but made her voice as sweet and light as she could. "Yes ma'am." She forced a smile on her face and skipped into the kitchen.

The woman stood behind a battered chair with her back to the door. Her cobweb gray hair was not in its usual bun, but was parted in the middle,and hung long down her back. She turned to take in the girl. Her thin lips curled up at the corners. "Look at the state of that hair, child. Full of snarls and tangles and—" the woman trailed off. *Naps*, thought the girl.

The woman gestured to the chair. The girl sat down, placed her brown hands on the white knees of her stockings. "Lean back," the woman said. The girl complied. The woman yanked back a section of the girl's hair with one hand. The teeth of the straightening comb slid in hot, prickling her scalp, and singeing out the kink.

The girl wrinkled her nose at the smell of burning hair. *Gramma Augusta always wore rings on her fingers.* The girl could not remember their colors. The woman sighed. "Soon, you'll have hair as pretty and straight as mine. Won't that be nice?"

"Yes," the girl said as the woman yanked back another handful. *What did Gramma Augusta's hands smell like after she made gumbo?*

"Yes, what?" The woman's tone was sharp with correction.

"Yes, Other Bee." The girl had learned that the woman would hear what she wanted to, as long as it was said sweetly.

"That's right, my darling Sarah. And soon you'll be as pretty as your Mother Bea." *Yank.*

I'm not Sarah, she thought, even if she could no longer remember the names Gramma Augusta called her. The woman dragged the comb through another section of hair. More burning, another memory singed away. The girl began to count the empty places inside her head, but had to stop when she got to twenty. She bit her lip, careful not to move her head as the hot comb passed her ear. *Not Sarah. Never be Sarah.*

When she was done, the woman stood back and said, "Stand up. Let me have a look, sweet Sarah." The girl stood and twirled, the skirt of her dress flaring out. The woman cooed. "Look at us, darling. Just like twins."

The girl looked over the woman's tall, austere figure. Even without a mirror, she knew her own nose was broader, her lips thicker, and her skin much darker than the Other Bee.

The doorbell rang. The Other Bee sighed once and went to the pantry. Pulled open the double doors. Grabbed a jar of honey from the middle shelf. "Just a moment, Sarah dear. There's a customer." The Other Bee strode down the hallway towards the front door, jar clutched close to her breast.

The girl looked into the open pantry. There were three shelves stocked with mason jars full of honey. Each jar was hand-labeled. On the very top shelf the jars had bright, red labels, and *that* honey the Other Bee never sold. Only used to sweeten her morning tea. On the second shelf were white-labeled jars she took with her to the door whenever someone rang. On the bottom shelf: blue-labeled jars with the honey she spooned into the girl's porridge and spread across the girl's toast in the afternoon.

Polite voices and pleasantries at the door echoed down the hall. The girl darted across the kitchen. She climbed onto to lowest shelf and steadied herself by nudging her hip against the wall. She grabbed a jar of the red-labeled honey, unscrewed the lid, and stuck a finger in. The front door cracked closed. She heard the turn of its lock. The girl screwed the lid back on the jar, then clambered down the shelves. She made a fist, hiding her honey-coated finger. She tiptoed across the kitchen floor and took her seat only seconds before the Other Bee returned to the kitchen.

"Are you hungry, dear heart? Shall I fix your breakfast?" The woman said, smoothing down an unruly lock of the girl's hair with a blue-veined hand. The girl *was* hungry. Her stomach rumbled. "No thank you, Other Bee. May I go outside and play?"

The woman smiled with colorless lips. "You are being very sweet today."

The girl cringed. *Could the woman tell what she had done?* The woman stroked her cheek. "Very sweet," she said. Her eyes were approving. She moved to shut the pantry.

The girl glanced behind her, saw Other Bee facing away, knew she had a moment where she wasn't being watched. She crammed her honeyed finger into her mouth. The honey was sharp and bright on her tongue. For a moment all the colors in the kitchen seemed richer.

She could smell the Other Bee's hand soap and shoe polish from across the kitchen. She licked a small trickle of honey from her palm.

"Tomorrow, I'll bring you some ribbons to tie up your hair." Other Bee said. She walked back over to the kitchen table and sat down across from the girl.

The girl turned in her chair to face her. "Can we get some for you, so we can always be like twins?"

Other Bee smiled. The lines around her eyes interlaced like spider-webs. She leaned over and kissed the girl on her forehead. Her lips were cold. "Yes, my dear one. We'll both wear ribbons in our hair."

"May I?"

"Play outside?" The woman's brow furrowed briefly, a suspicious look that quickly passed. "Of course, my love. But Mother has some work today. The bees will keep you company. They are industrious, good-hearted creatures. Not like the silly flowers; flowers only know how to lie."

The girl felt an itching behind her eyes. *Flowers.* She knew the flowers were important, but could not remember why. The girl kissed Other Bee on her papery cheek. "I'll do my best to play quietly so's not to interrupt."

"That's my good girl." The woman stood and unlocked the kitchen door.

The girl, stomach rumbling, sweetness on her lips, skipped out of the kitchen door into the garden's forking paths humming a joyful song. Her eyes did not smile. She knew the names of the flowers. Could tell the hydrangeas from snowball bushes at a glance. Could name the hardy hibiscus and false indigo and frangipani.

Throughout the garden's expanse were three white boxes, each containing a different hive of bees. The nearest was just beneath the girl's bedroom window. She stood for a minute in the sunlight, watching the bees in flight. She watched for a shadowed space where they did not busily attend the flowers and made for it, all the while humming her joyful song. In the shade of a willow, the girl bent over and brushed a purple hyacinth. She looked behind her. Satisfied that the Other Bee was not watching from the kitchen window, she whispered, "Tell me your story."

The Hyacinth bristled. "I knew a girl the color of sand. She loved a boy red-brown as the clay. The girl sang in the church. The most beautiful songs." The Hyacinth's star-shaped blossoms trembled and it began to sing. "'Get on board, children. For there's room for many-a-more!'"

The girl smiled. She had a flash of memory. A gray room with motes of dust dancing in the sunlight. A tall brown woman with round glasses in a long skirt singing those same words.

The Hyacinth murmured. "Clay-brown boy was a *sinner*. He never went to church. He missed the choir. Missed sand-colored girl's songs. But one day he was on a river fishing nearby the place sand-girl was doing the Monday washing. Heard a voice clear and strong and pure sing out. He forgot about his fish. Forgot about his pole. Knew he loved the singer. He loved sand-colored girl."

Other Bee's voice echoed in her head. *The plants will only tell you lies.* The girl stroked the Hyacinth's stem. "And did they kiss? Did they get married?"

The Hyacinth sighed long and low. "Purple Hyacinth only knows sorrow, child. If you would know my tale, understand that it is not a thing of happy endings."

The girl nodded. "But if you told only lies then the story you tell could be happy. If it is sad, it might be true. Tell me what happens?"

The Hyacinth continued. "They met at nights on the banks of the river. Their kisses were sweet and their eyes saw only each other. They made plans to run away and set up house.

"Sand girl's father was a minister. His skin was the color of beechwood. Minister's wife was the color of ashwood. She taught school. Neither would approve of their sweet, good daughter kissing that brown clay boy, who had no schooling and went on sinning far from church. So the girl and boy met together at dusk in secret, before the church bell rang, and before the school teacher had finished supper.

"Now, in those times there were riders. They wore all white and they brought death. They hated beechwood, sand, or ashwood. And even more they hated clay-brown, or the brown of the good earth, or the black of the night skies. In the dusk it's hard to see that sand is brown, not sugar white. And the riders came upon the brown boy and sand-colored girl, and saw their kisses and hated them. They thought the girl was one of their own, sugar-white, and they tied up the boy, and beat him, and took him to a sycamore tree.

"The girl wept and ran after them until her feet were bloody. But the riders laughed, and knocked her to the ground and hanged the boy from the tree. His hands and feet turned purple.

"The girl weeps by the river. Never sings her songs. And my flowers bloomed the purple of the boy's hands. This is my story."

The girl sobbed and knelt down in the dirt. Shaken by the unfairness of it she clenched her fists and pounded them into the earth. She whispered, "This must be true." She knew that Other Bee had lied to her again.

She wiped the tears from her eyes with the pinafore of her dress. "Hyacinth, can you tell me my name?"

The flower quivered. "I only know my story, child. Even the sand-colored girl's name is lost to me." The girl kissed the Hyacinth and said, "Thank you."

The girl wandered deeper into the garden, under trellises strewn with clematis. Across a bridge over a slow-moving stream choked with lotuses. Past jacaranda trees that showered her with purple-blue blossoms. They stuck in her hair and crunched beneath her feet. Each of these had their own stories, she knew, and they whispered and swayed in the wind. But their stories were not hers, and the songs they sang were unfamiliar.

She walked until she stood beneath the magnolia tree at the garden's heart. It towered above her; even if she craned her neck upwards she could see only the barest hint of sky between its dark, waxy leaves. Its huge white flowers were wider across than both her hands with her fingers spread. The girl sat down cross-legged on the grass beneath the tree and reached out to stroke its trunk. "Sister Magnolia, will you tell me your story?"

The branches of the tree shook. A solitary white flower as big as a teacup saucer drifted down from the tree's crown. The girl caught it, and cradled it gently in her hands. The voice from the blossom was deep, smooth, and sweet as cane syrup. "There was a gal used to sing the blues. She'd come home at night from waiting tables, and washing floors, and listen for the sounds of traffic to quiet. Then she'd sit at her table with its red-checked cloth. With her radio turned low, and the window opened wide, she'd sing to the moon. And the moon would sing back." The tree rumbled low and sad, in counterpoint to the flower. "Because the moon was lonesome in the sky, and just as weary as any table-waiting gal. They'd sing out their heartaches and tribulations. They were friends. The moon was that much less lonesome; so was the gal.

"But one night the moon lit the way to a fella in a fine felt hat, and a long winter coat. He heard the gal singing. The fella took her to sing out her heartache and tribulations on a stage lit up near as bright as the moon. She wore a dress that sparkled like the stars. Everyone who heard the gal sing loved her as much as the moon did. Soon the gal had a driver in a long moonbright car, and jewels and someone to wash her floors and bring her meals. The gal had love, and no more reason to sing the blues. But she missed her friend. Nightclubs had no place for the moon to sit, and the house band drowned out the moon's songs.

"So one night, wearing a string of pearls, each perfectly round and glowing, the gal walked straight off the stage, and went outside. Was a cloudy night, but she threw out her arms just the same. She sang out to the moon just as she did back in her cheap little room with its red and white checked table. The moon peeked through the clouds. Saw her old friend wearing little moons around her neck, singing their same old songs. The moon shone her light down and the gal glowed, so did a tree with night-dark leaves. Where the moon touched it, flowers big as any you ever did see, opened to touch the moonlight. 'For you,' the moon said.

"The moon gave my flowers to the gal; the gal gave her songs to the moon."

The girl tucked the magnolia flower into her hair, just above her ear. She remembered Gramma Augusta's wrists, dabbed with oil that smelled like magnolia, mingled with garlic, onion, and bell pepper. Those wrists and strong hands that glittered with rings. The girl remembered those hands setting flowers that looked like green-beaked birds with feathers made of fire in a vase. She said to the magnolia blossom, "You flowers only seem to have one story. But do you remember other flowers? You ever seen a flower that looks like a bird, all orange and blue and green?"

The magnolia blossom whispered, "From my highest bough I've seen a flower that looks like a bird. But it was cast down. Pushed beneath the earth."

The girl followed the garden's winding path past sunflowers whose bright yellow heads turned to follow her. Bees buzzed around ankle-level sea lavender. Dense perfume rose, disorienting her. Her limbs felt heavy.

"It's so hot." She said to no one. "Maybe if I just lie down beneath that tree." A mimosa tree stood just beyond the sea lavender. The shade of its pink and green canopy seemed to promise coolness and rest. Her tongue and lips tingled with a hint of remembered sweetness. She had only taken a foot off the path when the magnolia hummed in her ear. "It's just a little bit farther to the birds you was looking for."

The girl wiped sweat off her brow then put both feet firmly on the path. She clamped a hand over her nose and mouth. Weariness fled from her limbs. The bees' buzzing rose in pitch and menace. She ran along the path, pinching her nose shut with one hand, the other holding onto the magnolia in her hair. Bordering plants crowded onto the edges of the path. The girl ran past pink and red floribunda roses that snagged her skirt and pinafore with thorns. Panting, with a stitch in her side, she came to a high brick wall festooned with honeysuckle. A small patch of dark, damp smelling soil lay just before the wall. "Here," the magnolia said. The girl knelt down. The dampness of the earth soaked through the knees of her stockings. She rooted around in cool soil feeling for hidden plants or roots. After a time, she sat back on her heels and pulled out her hands. Tired, she wiped the dirt from her hands on the skirt of her dress. She looked at her thumb, still tender in the place she had bitten it. She squeezed it until she managed another drop of blood then flicked the blood onto the soil. Nothing happened.

The girl began to cry. *This was stupid.* "Bird flowers, I remember you. Nothing else in this whole garden stays underground. How can you?"

The soil churned and frothed like hot chocolate just off the stove. Green stalks poked through and up, each with a brilliantly orange-red crown of petals. Broad leaves unfurled like wings. The flowers preened. "We are the most magnificent of flowers: Strelitzia, the birds of paradise!"

The girl sniffled once, then wiped her nose on her sleeve. "I remember you. Please tell me your story."

The tallest of the flowers, with a petal as blue as the fire on the Other Bee's gas burners in his fan of orange-red, turned to regard her. "Can you not tell my story just by looking at me? Why are you not struck silent by my beauty?

"When the world began, it was a dance. And I was one of the dancers, the first child of the sun, the firebird. I burned brighter than the moon herself, and she was jealous of my beauty."

The magnolia scoffed and the bird-of-paradise stretched on its stalk. "Pardon, did I hear something?"

"Please don't stop your story," the girl said.

"As I was saying. My beauty was painful to gaze upon, but I burnt too bright. No flowers could grow, no rain could fall,and the earth was cracked and ugly. The moon whispered dark things to my mother the sun, and the sun was struck with compassion for the poor, dirty earth. She ordered clouds to form for rain, and she gave the earth a robe of green to cover itself, speckled with flowers to bring out beauty and color. Such beauty that the cracked, dry rock even outshone the moon. But such was my radiance that I would burn up the earth's new garments in an instant, so my mother transformed me into a mere plant, to take my place as the most beautiful of the flowers.

"Poor me, my beauty reined in, my heat taken. But one day, I will regain my true form and fly away from this ordinary ball of dirt in flame and glory!"

The girl smiled at this, but she remembered her grandmother and the table set with the birds-of-paradise, and the number of them that grew just outside her front window. They were beautiful, but no more so than the sweet pea that grew in a pot hanging from the back porch. She caressed one of the bird-of-paradise's leaves. "Wanna fly away from here, you and me? Ain't afraid of fire."

The crowned head of the plant seemed to sag. "Today is not the day for flame and glory."

The girl closed her eyes. She could remember the rings on her grandmother's fingers. Garnets, rubies, an amethyst, and a pearl that shone like the moon. She remembered her grandmother's voice. "Baby dumpling, your mama named you Cleopatra like the queen, and your great-grandma call you Cleo because you carry history. But to me you a baby dumpling, soft and sweet, near good enough to eat." She remembered laughing as Gramma Augusta tickled her ribs. She leaned over to kiss the bird-of-paradise. "Thank you, little firebird." The flower seemed to stand up a little straighter.

Cleo walked along the wall, pushing her hand through the creeping vines feeling for an opening in the brick. All around her she could hear the buzzing of bees.

After trampling through irises and crocuses, Cleo came to a place where one brick wall met another. There was a whitewashed wooden gate, half-hidden by Madagascar jasmine. Cleo pulled at it. It was locked. She kicked at it. The gate creaked loudly and groaned on its hinges. The buzzing of the bees grew louder. Cleo lowered her shoulder and prepared herself to take a run at the gate when she heard a voice from behind her. "Sarah darling, you've certainly been busy." The bees hummed in agreement.

Cleo turned around. The woman who called herself Mother Bea stood there, hands templed in front of her, cobweb-colored hair streaming behind her. Her eyes were shaded by the broad brim of a sun-hat. Her shoulders were bare. A bee landed on the woman's right shoulder, just covering a freckle. Cleo scowled. "All you do is lie. Who's Sarah?"

"I'm not sure I like your tone, young lady. Look, your hair's all a-tangle again."

"This is my hair. This is how it grows!"

"Young lady! This sort of tantrum is not at all becoming. If this is how you're going to behave when I allow you—"

"Allow nothin'! I look like me."

Mother Bea spread out her hands in supplication. Her fingers seemed far too long. "I trim and prune the plants. Water them, help them become their most beautiful. Should I do any less for you, my dear one?"

"I'm not a plant. I'm a girl." Cleo moved over to the gate and shook the latch.

The woman smiled her thin smile. Two more fat bees landed on her shoulder and a third hovered near her cheek. A vine from the Madagascar jasmine snaked out to wrap around Cleo's wrist. She shook it off. "Open the gate."

Bees wreathed the woman, covering her mist-colored dress, flitting in and out of her long cobweb hair.

"Ain't gonna scare me with your bees. I'll turn into smoke." Cleo kicked at the gate. Hard.

The bees intensified their buzzing. The woman laughed, not unkindly. "Smoke. You can't do that, Sarah."

"My name's not Sarah. It's Cleopatra Khadija Arceneaux. And it's Cleo and Baby Dumpling. But it ain't Sarah. And you don't know what I can do." Cleo kicked at the gate again. The wood splintered.

"I only want to keep you safe." The bees hummed with the woman's voice. "You can be my pretty daughter and I'll show you all the secrets of the garden, and one day it'll be yours."

Cleo kicked the gate. "I'm not your daughter." *Kick.*

"Sarah, sweetheart, the world outside is a terrible place. They won't care for you like I can. They won't protect you and love you. They can't teach you the things I can." The humming of the bees grew as her voice cracked and lost its characteristic smoothness. "Look how you came to my door, ragged and dirty, with a sad cardboard box of chocolate. I fed you. Clothed you. Burnt your rags."

"Those were play clothes, not rags!" Cleo slammed her body against the gate. "I was selling candy bars for a field trip. Gramma Augusta *never* let me go hungry."

Other Bee held out her arms for an embrace. The bees sounded frantic in their buzzing. Other Bee's eyes plead with Cleo. "The world is an unkind place for little girls. Especially little negro girls. Even ones with your gifts."

"Maybe the world is a bad place." Cleo sighed, knowing that some of what the Other Bee said was true. "Maybe it's mean. But I'll be badder and meaner if I have to. You can't keep me here."

The gate crashed open. The bees dispersed in a cloud from Other Bee, who looked frail and tired. The Madagascar jasmine looked brown at the edges. The sun hat was in her hands. She had tears in the corner of her eyes. "If you leave here, you can never come back. Stay for just a little longer, and I'll teach you how to grow fire strawberries and the sweet fig of wisdom. This place is safe from the ways of the world. Only I can give you this safety." The woman brushed Cleo's cheek with one of her long fingers. "I won't comb your hair anymore. Just stay."

"No," Cleo said.

She stepped out of the garden and closed the gate behind her. Beyond Other Bee's enclosed space, the air was cool. Ordinary smells: car exhaust, cat piss, the garlicky odor of the Chinese delivery place down the street, assailed Cleo. She let out a bark of joy; she was on her own street. The sun had just set; the sky to the west was a lurid rose-gold that dripped over the hills and deepened into black.

The sidewalk in front of the Other Bee's bungalow had buckled and cracked where the roots of a ficus had tunnelled beneath. The streetlights glowed, muting the reds and yellows of the cars on the street. Ahead of her, only four doors down, was her grandmother's house. Its porch light still lit for her. She wiped her eyes with the back of her hand. Gramma Augusta would be so worried.

Cleo had never stayed out past the streetlights' first glow. Would Gramma yell? Would she cry? Would she ground Cleo for a month? Behind her the thick, sweet smell of tuberose lingered. Cleo made her way home over the broken sidewalk, holding onto the magnolia tucked in her hair, careful not to step on any cracks. She did not look back.

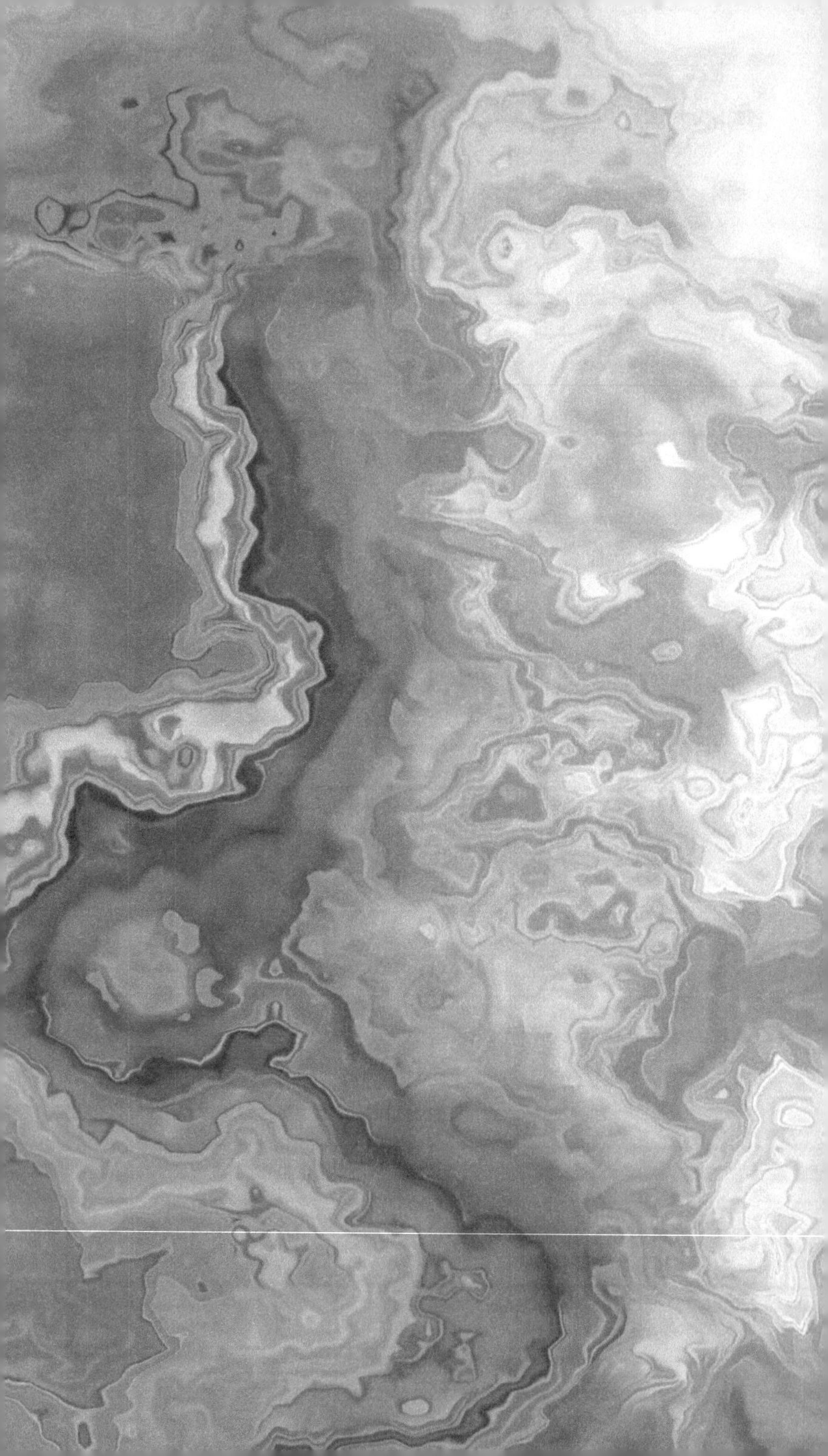

Serving Fish

ERIC RAN TOWARDS the shore of the lake, still half
made-up as Mahogany Eternique, heels in hand,
gaffing tape undone, red taffeta train dragging behind
in the mud. He sprinted until he reached the water's
edge, picking up speed despite snagging his dress twice
on branches that littered the shore, and fell to his knees.
The cool water soaked through all four pairs of pantyhose
as it lapped against his knees and calves. Panting, and
clutching the side which ached from running a mile
and a half in a corset, Eric tried to work up enough spit
to speak without croaking. His nostrils flared wide. He
breathed in the dank, algae smell of lake water.

He licked his lips, glitter rough against his tongue, and pitched his voice as loud as he dared across the water. "Flounder, flounder in the sea, rise up from the depths for me..."

He stared across the surface of the lake for nearly a minute, watching the city lights reflect. Except for a few leaves washing up onto the shore, the water seemed untroubled. Eric called out over the water again, his voice cracking with expectation, "Flounder, flounder in the sea?"

But the lake's surface remained placid. He stared across the water for what felt like forever, not daring to blink. At last, Eric shuddered, and shut his eyes. A great spasm shook his body. Tears mixed with mascara clumped like oil droplets in his false eyelashes.

A rasping baritone rose above the sound of the cars behind and the water lapping against the shore ahead. "This is not, strictly speaking, a sea."

Eric's eyes snapped open. An enormous black shape lay just beneath the lake's surface. It's grown as big as an eighteen wheeler, Eric thought. The front end of an immense flatfish, scaly and covered in barnacles broke the surface. Two jaundiced eyes the size of dinner plates on the same side of a misshapen head regarded him; a sideways mouth opened and closed, spiny teeth gnashing in the air. Eric straightened his back, his bodice sagging against his chest without the padding he used to fill it, and spread out his arms in supplication. "Though you may not care for my request, I've come to ask it, nonetheless."

The sideways mouth opened, and the voice echoed over the water. "I wondered when you would ask again. What is it this time?"

Eric's eyes glittered dangerously. "Revenge."

The yellow eyes seemed to wobble slightly. "You know the costs."

Eric smiled sadly. "I do."

The surface of the lake roiled, and a sudden salty wind sprang up from nowhere, stinging Eric's cheek and eyes.

The baritone voice cracked out up over the howling wind as the giant fish sank down into whatever depths it had come from.

"Granted."

WHEN ERIC WAS ten, his parents, deciding that he needed to toughen up and be more of a man, sent him on a long crabbing and fishing trip with his grandparents. Nestled in the plush back seat of his grandmother's rust-colored Chevrolet Caprice, Eric read facts about Pacific marine life from the backs of collectible cards with glossy colored photos while his grandfather fumed about the traffic from Sacramento to Bodega Bay. "I don't know why these fools even get in cars if they can't drive."

Eric's grandmother sucked at her dental bridge; it gave her a sour look. "Roland, you pull over at the next stop and I'll drive the rest. Doctor said to mind your blood pressure."

"My blood pressure'll be fine. Wait'll we get to the boats. Sea air and a reel will fix us up. Maybe straighten the naps out of that boy's hair."

"Roland. Leave him alone."

"I just don't get why his mama let his hair get wild like that. He needs a military cut. Don't know where that nappy hair comes from, not my side."

Eric's grandmother sucked at her bridge again. "Quit pretending you had good hair before you lost it and drive if you're going to. I'm going to rest my eyes."

Eric read about the mating habits of the grunion. His grandfather turned up the radio and grunted in approval at the Stylistics. Eyelids heavy, lulled by the sounds of classic R&B, Eric fell asleep.

When he awoke, it was twilight and the Caprice was parked in front of a weathered motel that had seen better days.

The seafoam green door to room seven was ajar, and his grandfather bustled in carrying luggage and a tackle box. His grandmother was still sitting in the front, and patted him on the cheek. "You hungry? I brought some red beans in Tupperware. I'll heat 'em up on the hotplate if you want something to eat."

Eric nodded and slid bonelessly out of the car, and trudged into room seven, wiping his feet on the mat and staring at the swirls on the carpet. They were the colors of pea soup and chocolate milk. The motel room smelled like the sea and old cigarettes. Eric lay down on the double bed closest to the window without taking off his Keds and stretched his arms out wide as if to fill as much space as possible. His grandmother poured a grey-brown mass of red beans and hamhocks into a little pot on the hot plate and hummed softly. Eric fell asleep to the sounds of the sea and his grandmother's wordless hymn.

The next morning, they went out on a mostly white fishing boat named "Aphrodite's Kiss" with a small group of retirees who seemed to regard the serious-faced, slight black boy with a mixture of amusement and wariness. One of them, an elderly man with an impressive mustache and wispy remnants of sideburns smiled at Eric with nicotine-stained teeth and asked, "Looking forward to a battle of nature on the high seas?"

Eric shook his head and fingered the pair of binoculars around his neck. "No sir. I hope we won't be fighting nature. I'm on nature's side."

The old man laughed and clapped Eric on the back. "This one's a regular John Muir."

After about a half hour, the boat found a still, quiet place on the ocean, and the crew cut the engines. Fishing reels came out. Eric's grandmother helped him bait his hooks with shrimp flies. "This one works especially well on sand dab, Baby Dumplin'."

Eric tried not to blush at the nickname and focused

on attaching a two-pound sinker to his line. With his grandmother watching approvingly from over his shoulder, he cast off and waited. His grandmother leaned in close enough that he could smell her, a mixture of Oil of Olay, baby powder, and designer imposter perfume, over the salt smell of the sea. "Remember, sand dabs bite a bunch of times then stop. Don't pull 'em up the first time you get a bite. You gotta be patient."

Eric nodded, rested his chest against the railing, and felt the boat bob up and down on the waves. Overhead, seabirds whirled and screamed. The men sometimes punctuated the quiet with raucous laughter at jokes told at a volume too low for Eric to hear.

One by one the retirees reeled in their catch. Wriggling flat fish with eyes on the left sides of their heads flopped on the deck as they were brought up and pulled off hooks. The fish were tan and mottled like the backs of the retiree's hands. Eric kept his hand steady on his rod as he watched his grandfather drop six pancake-sized fish into a bucket. Minutes passed without so much as a tremble on his line from the rising ocean breeze.

Eric's grandmother patted his shoulder after stopping to pluck some fish from her own hook. "Not everyone is lucky all the time."

But then the end of his rod bowed down nearly an inch. His fingers tingled and itched, but remembering what his grandmother had told him, he waited. The line jerked seven times in rapid succession, then lay still. He began to reel in the line, eyes gleaming with triumph. He turned the handle, slowly at first, but faster as he felt the weight on the end of line. His grandfather squinted and peered over his shoulder, "Looks like you caught a nice dab or three, boy."

He turned the handle as smoothly as he could manage, although his arms ached from the effort. After what seemed an interminable period, a flatfish wider than Eric's head splashed through the surface wriggling on the end of his line.

He whooped and brought it down on the deck with a
fleshy thump. But when he leaned over to pull it from the
hook, the world went quiet.

The air around him was still, and all the adults seemed
taken by a spontaneous game of freeze tag. Eric blinked
twice and rubbed his eyes. The fish was still wriggling.
It opened its sideways mouth and spoke to him in a voice
that was low and rasping. "Only you can hear me, boy. I
slowed things down so we'd have a chance to talk."

"Fish don't talk." Eric set his jaw and glared
suspiciously behind him. The adults were still motionless.

The fish flopped and made a rasping noise that might
have been a laugh. "But yet I speak. Look, I wasn't always
a fish. I'll spare you the details. I was once a man. If you
throw me back in the sea, you'll have my gratitude. And
my help if I can give it."

"What kind of help? Can you grant wishes?"

"Nothing so crude. But I can change things that are to
things that are not, if you ask. Doing so will come with a
cost, though."

The boy exhaled sharply. He had just read The
Monkey's Paw in class. "What if I decide not to throw you
back and forget about all this magic and stuff?"

The rasping sound again. "Then I get fried up, or eaten
with butter and lemon, and you lose a chance to touch
mystery."

"I'm going to throw you back, but not because I want
magic or to be a detective or anything like that. But 'cause
you can talk."

"Very well. But the offer stands if you change your
mind. If you need my help, stand at the shore of the ocean
and call, 'Flounder, flounder in the sea, come up from the
depths for me,' and I will aid you as best as I can."

"Aren't you a sand dab?"

Rasp. Eric picked up the fish with both hands and
threw it over the side. A thin red ribbon of blood trailed

behind it through the water. Eric was so still that he did not notice that movement around him had resumed. His grandfather grumbled, "What you do a fool thing like letting that nice piece of fish go?"

"Roland, leave the boy alone," his grandmother said.

"Fine. But he don't get none of my fish. He can eat red beans again."

DURING HIGH SCHOOL, Eric fell in with a group of queer kids who played butch in front of their peers. He was adopted one day after yearbook class by Events Editor Phil, who eyed him and asked conversationally, "You like guys, don't you?"

Taken aback by the bluntness of the question, Eric could think to do nothing else but nod, and soon after found himself completing a trio that ran havoc on the seedy streets of Los Angeles.

Each of them adopted fake names for their clandestine lives; Phil called himself Lucky hoping that it would ring true, Nico chose the name Ram in a none-too-subtle advertisement of his sexual proclivities, and Eric's slight figure and beatific expression earned him the nickname Angel. Phil and Nico's parents relaxed whenever they saw Eric around; they were certain a good boy like that would keep their own wild children out of trouble.

On Friday nights, Eric would go with Lucky and Ram to The Study, a seedy gay bar in Hollywood that seldom checked ID. Ram liked rough trade, and there was a certain kind of thug that lingered over the too-strong drinks served up by the Korean bartender regulars called Chinese Andy. One Friday, just before the Spring term ended, Eric sat at the bar primly, hands in lap, sipping a throat-scorching Cuba Libre that had only the barest hint of Coca-Cola.

Ram was in the back parking lot, probably pressed against the wall by some hard-living gangster who couldn't resist a bit of muscular teenage flesh. Andy kept an eye on Eric whenever Ram or Lucky wandered off, shooing anyone who got too close with a pestilential stare and pointed references about chicken not being on the menu.

This Friday wasn't especially busy, and Eric passed the time arguing with Andy about books they'd read. "I still think there's something deeply creepy about how Marq manipulates Rat Korga," Eric said, gesticulating a little with his right hand.

Andy shrugged and wiped down the counter with a rag, scrubbing at an ancient stain. "So you think it's really about a 'good' slave master? I just think it's hot."

The red padded front door slammed open as if to punctuate Andy's opinion. Eric whipped his head around to take in the figure filling the door: 6'4" in heels and sequins with towering wig and nails sharp as talons stood the biggest, baddest, blackest drag queen Eric had ever seen. For a moment the queen stood stock still, posed like an Old Hollywood Vamp and seemed to shimmer like the haze over the asphalt on the hottest summer day. Eric felt something new well up inside him. Not lust, covetousness. The drag queen seemed to evoke an unearthly, titanic beauty, like a Valkyrie covered in stardust and come to land in the pothole-filled parking lot of The Study. Then the spell was broken as the queen laughed and shouted out in basso profundo, "Chinese Andy! A girl can work up a thirst. Make mama a whisky sour."

It was that same year that Ram had the brilliant idea for the lot of them to rent a U-Haul truck and ride in the back to beach party in Malibu. Eric had misgivings. "I don't think it'll be safe."

Ram slapped him on the back. "It'll be fine! All six of us can't fit in Lucky's shitty Stanza. Think of it like a limo. Without windows."

"Don't think limousines use lawn chairs as seating." Lucky said, worrying a kiss curl into another position on his forehead.

Ram smirked. "Limos also don't let teenagers drink Ram's famous Malibu cocktails out of a gallon jug."

"Still sounds dangerous. No seatbelts," Eric said, peering into the gloomy interior of the truck.

Ram put his hand on his forehead mockingly. "Oh la, poor Angel is such a delicate china doll he would just break to pieces if we hit a bump in the road." Then, scowling, "Nigga, just because you high yella don't mean you ain't got warrior blood. You can see them African naps fightin' on your head."

Eric took a long swig from the jug of fruit punch and rum then clambered into the back of the truck with four others, muttering under his breath. Ram pulled the sliding door closed with a slam and darkness closed in on them. "The Elegance!" Eric shouted.

Except for being knocked around as the truck navigated turns and a moment of terror as Eric's lawn chair nearly collapsed under him, the half hour drive to Malibu was uneventful. When Ram pulled open the sliding door, the gallon of punch was more than half-finished between the four of them in the back, and they all blinked and squinted in the daylight.

Ram bowed with mock-gallantry, "My Ladies, your chariot has arrived."

Eric frowned. "I feel like I've been in a rock tumbler."

"You're no longer a diamond in the rough then," Lucky said.

Eric hopped out of the back of the truck, gathered what dignity he had left, and turned to take in the sights. The pale sands stretching beneath a stony promontory were covered with towels, pavilions, beach umbrellas, and folding chairs of a dizzying variety of candy colors. And the people! Black men, women, and drag queens of every size, shape, and shade from inky to ivory cavorted, posed, and preened by the shore. A towering coffee-and-cream colored drag queen in a feathered showgirl headdress was playing beach volleyball against a blue-black muscle-boy in speedos who couldn't have been more than five feet tall. A slender caramel-colored boy walked arm-in-arm with his dark chocolate boyfriend. Eric stood there trying to take it all in. Ram rumbled over his shoulder, "Girl, close your mouth before something flies in. We need to find a place to set down so haters can break their necks looking at us."

Ram strode towards the shore like a peacock, glaring at anyone who bothered to smile. Eric followed behind half-smiling, holding the half-empty container of punch. Lucky ululated in imitation of savages from bad movies and tromped puppyish over the sands, innocent of ugly looks and curses when he his passing scattered sand onto blankets and beach towels.

After they set up an umbrella and Ram lay out to drink up the sun in the sluttiest pose he could devise, Eric crept away from the group toward a narrow line of rock at the far edge of the shore. From there he could take in everything, the ocean, the dazzling people, the rich deep color of it all without worrying that he was too colorless by comparison.

From his perch on the rock, he saw the crowd part as if royalty was approaching. Standing nearly a head taller than everyone around her was Ebony Eternique, the drag queen he had first glimpsed months ago at The Study. She wore a rhinestone spangled gold bikini, a translucent cape and the highest Lucite heels Eric had ever seen. Her wig was arranged in a tower of gleaming curls dusted through with pearls and crystals. Despite her mass, she seemed to glide effortlessly. Her platform heels glittered in the sun and did not seem to sink in the sand. The wind blew her chiffon cape behind her and almost every eye was on her in admiration or envy. She was no mere queen anymore, but a Goddess, Venus in reverse come to wade inexorably into the sea.

Eric's heart beat fast, and his mouth tasted like chalk. Makeup, baubles, and poise had given Ebony power. This was magic. This was mystery. Mystery. The word struck a chord in his memory. He thought of a childhood trip to Bodega Bay, of a sand dab he'd caught and abandoned. With a sad, drunken smile, he turned his face away from the party and towards the sea spray. In little more than a whisper he called, "Flounder, flounder in the sea, come up from the depths for me..."

The world went still.

Seagulls froze in midflight. The water roiled and turned black. The sand dab surfaced. The flatfish had grown as big as a manhole cover. Much too large for that species of fish, Eric thought, remembering his animal cards.

It swiveled its froggy eyes towards him. The sideways mouth seemed to grin. "It's been a long time. Seven years? I thought you gave up on magic."

"I want to BE magic, like Ebony Eternique."

The fish wriggled. "You've been drinking."

Eric shrugged. "You said you could help me."

The fish made the rasping sound that might be a laugh. "I can give you the power to transfix men, to fascinate them with your gaze. I can give you the power to rule hearts. But it will cost."

"I don't have a lot of money."

The fish rasped. "Not that sort of cost. You will become a little more like me, and a little less like you. This is the cost."

Eric shrugged. "That doesn't sound so bad."

The flesh between his toes grew cold and began to itch. He felt skin pulled taut and stretch. He looked down in sudden horror as webbing knitted his toes together like a fin.

The fish sank beneath the waves. Its baritone echoed out from behind Eric. "Granted."

The noise of the world returned again.

IT TOOK ERIC nearly a month to work up the nerve to talk to Ebony Eternique about drag, and then almost another two after that to ask if Ebony could show him how to be a drag queen. Ebony had grabbed Eric's face with her strong, long fingers and stared at him for twenty seconds in the dim light of The Study before sucking her teeth, laughing and slapping Eric hard on the back. "I never had a drag baby, but there's something about you. Sure, I'll be your mama."

At first it seemed hopeless. Eric was terrible at doing his own makeup, awful at lip synching, and clumsy in heels. But Ebony didn't give up, and neither did Eric. And after she drilled him to the point where he could walk backwards down stairs in heels, do contour makeup in his sleep, and lip synch to songs in languages he couldn't speak, Ebony decided her protégé was ready.

Eric was set to make his debut at Diamond Catch, a notorious gay nightclub whose patrons were not at all shy about voicing their displeasure with substandard acts. He had run through a dress rehearsal earlier in the week, but that night was his first time in front of a crowd.

Three songs before he was scheduled to go on, he waited backstage with Ebony, who was going on just before him. Backstage was a cramped, crowded storeroom filled with musty costumes, cracked mirrors, and queens in various states of undress.

A skinny, pockmarked boy with frizzy hair and prominent front teeth was slathering on foundation furiously. Eric smiled tentatively. The boy put his hands on his hips. "I hope you don't bomb. I'm supposed to go on after you, and I'm still cooking. Buy me some time."

Eric adjusted his wig in the mirror. "I hope I don't either. I'm Eri—Mahogany."

"Eri-Mahogany? That's a bougie name. I am Sierra Sin. You may call me Mistress." Sierra turned to glance at Eric. "Well. You are most definitely a fishy queen. You look like a real girl. I bet you'll get all kinds of chasers."

"Chasers?"

Sierra snorted. "Don't you know nothing? 'Straight' boys who want to hit some of that ass you got padded."

Ebony called over her shoulder as she stomped toward the stage. "My baby ain't takin' up with no trash. And daylight is no queen's friend, so she'll be keeping that face in the night."

Eric looked at himself in the mirror again. His balls ached from being tucked out of sight, his feet were sore, the padding was hot, and his face was caked with makeup, but the illusion was startling. Mahogany was a goddess like Dorothy Dandridge or Lena Horne. Mahogany glided over to wait in the wings while Ebony performed her set.

All too soon, Ebony finished her lip synch, and gestured towards Mahogany. The basso profundo voice seemed to fill the world. "And I have a very special treat for y'all. My little baby is going to tear up the stage tonight for you, for the first time. Give it up for Mahogany Eternique!"

Mahogany prowled out onto the stage like a leopard, drinking up the spotlight that shimmered on her sequins. She could do this. Men were creatures for her to control. The music welled up behind her, and her lips took the shape of the words. Her eyes sought out a man and she thought, *want*. The sudden heat was palpable. She knew he'd do anything for her, and she reached out her hand and smiled contemptuously as he fumbled in his wallet to pass her a twenty dollar bill. One by one, she ensnared them with her smoldering gaze, making them feel her beauty. The crowd crushed against the stage trying to get close to her. She gave none of them a second glance until her gaze settled on someone who she didn't need to inflame. Andy. Eric's eyes lingered on his friend with a newfound understanding. Then the song ended, the lights came up, and he exited to thunderous applause.

FOUR YEARS AFTER the beach party, Lucky had moved across country to go to college, Ram had found Jesus, gone back to being Nico, and turned into an enormous pain in the ass. But Eric kept in touch with Andy, who came to almost every one of his shows as Mahogany. Mahogany Eternique was doing three shows a week at two different clubs and making more than enough in tips and her cut of the door to pay the rent as well as foot the bill for wigs, makeup, accessories, and the fabric needed to create new and ever more outré costumes.

At least once a month he and Andy would make time to have dinner together. Eric would leave Mahogany behind in her world of wigs, makeup, and lip synch to talk to Andy about books someplace where no one paid any attention to him.

One month they went to Santa Monica Pier for dinner. Not any particular restaurant. Eric grabbed a corn dog, and Andy got fish and chips from a stand. They walked along the pier past the carnival games talking. Andy stuffed a ketchup-soggy fry into his mouth. "Hey, you want to try some of this? It's surprisingly good."

Eric shook his head. "I hate fish."

Andy smirked. "That's something I expect Mahogany to say. She wouldn't eat her own kind."

Eric shook his head. "Just because I serve fish realness three times a week doesn't mean I feel like being at the top of the food chain."

Andy stuffed a bit of fried cod into his mouth. "Your loss. Hey, wanna do that test your strength thing?"

"I'll win."

Seven carnival games and three stuffed animals later, the two of them sat in companionable silence on a bench overlooking the ocean. Darkness had settled in somewhere between the water-gun races and the darts. Andy put an arm around Eric. "It's weird. I hated that job at The Study, but meeting you came out of it, so being called Chinese for a year-and-a-half was worth it."

Eric smiled. "I'm glad you were there to keep me from being kidnapped by some OG with a thing for girly-boys."

Andy stirred. "I always loved this place. It reminds me of being a kid. Reminds of when I thought everything would work out all right, you know?" He slumped forward and his shoulders sagged.

"Hey? Something up?" Concern limned Eric's eyes.

Andy sighed. "Yeah. My mother. She's a tough old bird. But the cancer's come back, again. And each time the chemo's worse." His voice cracked. "I don't know if she can handle it again."

Eric turned to face Andy and squeezed his shoulder. "You got friends who love you. We're there for you."

Andy leaned in to kiss Eric. Eric kissed back, parting his lips, crushing them against Andy's teeth. The stubble on Andy's chin scraped against the smoothness of Eric's skin. Yes, Eric thought. He was hungry for this. Then, abruptly Eric pulled back.

Andy's eyes widened in confusion. His cheeks were still flushed and lips plump with arousal. "Is there something wrong?"

Eric smiled and covered Andy's hand with his own. "No everything's okay, I just need some air." He stood up and half-stumbled away from the bench.

Eric walked to the edge of the pier, a balloon tied to his left wrist, holding a teddy bear in his right hand. He looked over the railing at the black water below with the lights from the Ferris wheel and the carnival rides reflecting back like a parody of the night sky. He called out over the shrill music of the carousel and the popping of airguns, "Flounder, flounder in the sea, come up from the depths to me…"

The music cut mid-note. This time the sand dab loomed in the surf as big as a Volkswagen bug.

"Four years. Doing better than most. I imagine that little trick I taught you got some use?"

"What can you do about someone who's dying?" Eric shouted, although the world was still and quiet.

"I cannot resurrect the dead. But dying is another matter. I can cure someone who is ill. But there is always the cost."

"I need you to heal Andy's mother! Fuck the costs." Eric shouted. He felt an itching and a coldness down his left arm. Then pain in pinpricks. He rolled up the sleeve of his shirt in time to see iridescent scales push themselves through his skin to lie down flush like tiles along his arm.

The fish sank beneath the waves. "Granted."

ANDY MOVED TO Denver about a year after his mother went into spontaneous remission. Eric and Andy kept in touch, although Mahogany's schedule remained full, and grew fuller as drag returned to mainstream attention via reality shows. Mahogany went on tour, and after a packed show before a Denver audience, Eric met with Andy for dinner at an all-night taco joint.

While nibbling on a carne asada taco with extra chile verde, Andy remarked, "I'm not used to seeing you all glamorous for dinner."

Eric, still made up as Mahogany, laughed. "I'm not crazy about it, but I went straight from the airport to the club where I did my makeup for three hours, and I'm famished." He illustrated this by cramming an entire carnitas taco into his mouth without smudging his lipstick.

Andy whistled. "If I knew you had such skills, I mighta hit that."

Eric slapped him playfully on the upper arm. "You had your chance."

After dinner they walked arm-in-arm together along the banks of the Platte River, laughing and remembering old times. Eric's eyes were luminous and sad. "Sometimes I feel like you're the only one I can be real with, Andy."

"Even dressed like this?" Andy squeezed one of Eric's birdseed breasts.

As they walked past stoner hill, a figure lurched out of the bushes. The sodium glare of the streetlights did him no good. He was fifty-ish and squat. He had a Fu Manchu style mustache that made his mouth look droopy and petulant. His greasy Jheri Curl hair reminded Eric of seaweed.

Eric clutched Andy's hand nervously; the strange man was carrying a crowbar in his right hand, and a car stereo in the left. The man's skin was pockmarked and his shoe-leather brown complexion had an ashy grey undertone to it.

"We don't want any trouble," Andy said, holding his hands out.

The man smiled. He held out the car stereo. "Y'all want to buy this? Like brand new. Only been used once."

Andy shook his head. "Naw man. We don't want to buy stolen goods."

The man slurred, "Why you think it's stolen? You think you better than me?" His eyes narrowed at Andy. "You gooks always tryin' to steal good black women with your one-inch peckers."

Eric curled his hands into fists. "Not a woman, bruh. Leave us be."

The man's face contorted and he spat on the ground. "Faggot!"

He moved towards Eric with surprising swiftness.

Panicking, Eric projected desire at the man. *Want.* The man's eyes widened for a moment and his jaw went slack. Then his face contorted again and he slammed his crowbar into Andy's face. The crunching sound was sickening, and as Andy slid to the ground, Eric fell to his knees in horror.

It was a precious few moments before Eric could compose himself enough to call 911.

AFTER AN AMBULANCE took Andy away, and the police had questioned Eric and promised an APB, Eric found himself in the blue-grey waiting room of the Trauma Unit at the nearest hospital. Half-dressed and all numb he stared at a cup of hot chocolate someone had brought him hours ago. It had gone cold and congealed. His lipstick was still perfect.

A tired-eyed doctor in faded orange scrubs hovered at Eric's shoulder. "You were Andrew Kim's friend?"

The "were" in that sentence slammed down in Eric's chest like a stone. He stood up, poised with his head held high, and walked towards the door. He did not wait to hear the doctor say, "I'm sorry."

Outside of the sliding doors to Emergency an EMT was taking a furtive smoke break. Eric walked near him and forced a smile. "Hey, what's the nearest body of water? Big body of water?"

"Sloan's Lake," the EMT pointed vaguely north, "That way a ways. But it's not safe at night. Especially dressed like that."

Eric broke out into a run.

AFTER THE FISH sank into the murk of Sloan Lake, Eric stood and felt tiny pinpricks all along his spine.

Good, he thought. He sniffed the air particles wafting above: gasoline, sweat, cheap tacos from the down the road. He opened his mouth, ran a tongue over sharp barbed teeth that had sprouted just behind the set he had capped, cleaned, and straightened after adolescence. Without knowing how he knew, he knew where his prey was. Swifter than he would have thought possible, he darted along the shore and headed inexorably towards Federal Boulevard. He avoided cars and early morning pedestrians.

There. Across the street from him was a little yellow house. A Chevy Impala stood on blocks in the driveway. He knocked on the door forcefully three times. He heard stirring. The door creaked open on its chain. Fury rose up in Eric, its intensity driving all color from the world. The same piggy eyes. The Jheri Curl. The stupid Fu Manchu mustache. He forced his snarl into a smile and projected at the man. *Want.*

The man's face slid into a lazy smile. "So, you came here without your gook? You wanna play? I'll tap that ass if you can keep it on the downlow, baby."

Eric made his hips sway. He lowered his eyelids and parted his lips. "Oh, I got something that will sho' nuff set your world on fire."

The man rubbed his crotch. "Well hurry in baby, before someone sees you." He opened the door wide enough for Eric to slide in.

The door shut behind them with a slam. He grabbed Eric's ass and kneaded it. "I knew a bitch like you would want some of this."

"Yes," Eric said into his ear, feeling his new teeth lengthen. "What do I call you, Daddy?"

"Mm. Daddy. Yeah. Big Daddy is just right. Big Daddy got something for that ass." He slid his hand up from Eric's ass to reach for the zipper on his dress. Spines soundlessly ripped through the taffeta, and dripping with fluid, rose to meet Big Daddy's hand.

"Ow! The fuck!" he cried.

Eric shoved him back and opened his mouth. Human teeth cascaded to the floor, revealing sharp, spiny, barbed things.

Big Daddy screamed in terror, even while clutching his hand that had already begun to swell and purple.

"His name was Andy, not gook, you fuck."

Eric walked out the door, stately as if in a procession, even as he felt the cold, familiar prickling of scales sprout up his right arm. He ignored Big Daddy's howls of fury as he turned back towards Sloan Lake, trailing the tatters of his red dress behind him.

The skin between his fingers itched and tightened as they fused into fins. Once clear of the Impala, he broke into a run, not out of fear, not in fury, but for the sheer joy of it, even as the skin beneath his jaw opened up and feathery gills sprouted.

He returned to Sloan Lake, gasping for breath from a mouth twisting sideways, fell into the water with a resounding splash and disappeared beneath the surface, leaving only a ribbon of taffeta red as blood behind him.

If Salt Lose Its Savor

R ESTLESS AND TROUBLED by salt-dreams, Dion was up before dawn.

The night workers in the dryhouse sang work songs. Dion yoked her buckets across her shoulders and waded out into the sea, the face of the waters still black and littered with reflected stars. Red bands across the eastern sky shot through heavy clouds that threatened a storm. She closed her eyes, feeling the waters slap against her thighs. Underneath there was a glimmer of something, like light. She waded out until the feeling made her whole body tingle, and then bent her knees, filling her buckets with sea water.

This season had been hard. Perhaps it could still turn sweet at the end. She trudged back to shore and turned her buckets into the first of three big terracotta jars. She repeated this, waiting for the tingle each time. The sun rose higher in the sky. The other women—refiners, harvesters, kit-girls, and runners—all filled the beach with noise and nervous energy.

KYA, ONE OF Dion's two kit-girls, was waiting for her on a return trip to the shore. Dion dumped her buckets into her jar and knelt on the sand. Kya wiped her brow with a cloth and held up a dish of cool, fresh water for Dion drink from.

"Beaucourt coming in two days." Kya said, her round eyes in a round brown face softening her look of disapproval. "Be a sore shame to disappoint him with salt ain't barely blue."

"Only us that makes the salt, girl. He can be disappointed. Nowhere else for him to buy."

"Only him that buys it."

When Dion had started harvesting salt—a girl not much older than Kya—there had been no fewer than eight magicians all vying for the bluest and purest. Now there was only the Beaucourt.

Dion jutted her chin at the nearly full harvest pot. "My right palm itching at this here."

Kya squinted. "For true? Mama Gwe says your itching ain't never led us wrong."

Dion nodded, and spit onto the sand. "Could even be some of the true lapis."

A spatter of raindrops struck them on the shoulders.

Dion shouted, "Nashi!"

Her other kit-girl sidled out from the inside of the dryhouse, with a guilty look and a mouth full of cornbread.

Dion nodded. "Rain's starting. We got to get this harvest ready for drying."

Dion helped the girls filter the harvested water through rough, untinted linen into broad porcelain pans. Each girl hurried the pans inside to the firepits. Olu wood smoke and steam rose in a fragrant pillar where Nashi's pan slopped over into the fire.

"Careful, girl," Dion scolded. "One plash of the true lapis is worth four of you."

Dion carried the third and fourth pans in herself. Her rolling walk was easy. She did not spill a drop.

WHEN DION GOT home, Aya stood at the table kneading dough for tomorrow's bread. Dion wrapped her arms around her wife. Pressed her nose into a space at the nape of her neck. Aya relaxed into the embrace, her powerful arms pounding and pulling the dough. "Wasn't expecting you home until after dark. Chicken ain't ready." Aya glanced at an iron pot hanging over the hearth. Dion could smell the chicken, herbs, and groundnuts simmering. Her stomach rumbled.

Aya slapped the bread dough, covered it and left it to rise. Dion rested her chin in the crook of Aya's shoulder.

"You was up early," Aya said.

"Mm. Salt-dreams. Didn't want to wake you."

Aya broke the embrace, turned to face Dion. She wiped flour from hands on the front of her apron. "A lot of those lately, beloved. You been harvesting longer than you rightly ought to."

"My Big Mama harvested her whole life, near. She be out there now if the Grey Barons ain't take her."

"And your Auntie Pru? The one was sensitive? Like you? How long she manage?"

Dion looked away. "This been a hard season. We wasn't gonna make enough silver to put away. But if I ain't wrong, I may have pulled some of the true lapis. Be enough to stop me arguing with you about working."

Aya sighed. "Alls I wants is a tough old bird in the pot, and you to keep me warm at night. Don't need silks. Don't need lamb."

Dion said, "Not aiming for a fortune. Just enough so you can have that tough old bird, maybe get a pot mended without worrying how we gonna make it through a fortnight."

"These dreams of things that happened, or things still to come?"

Dion shook her head. "Don't rightly know. They wicked. Don't leave me with no rest."

Aya's gaze softened. "Sit down. I'll knot your hair."

Dion sat by the hearth. Aya knelt over her, parting and knotting her hair with her fingers until Dion fell asleep.

DION FOUND HERSELF in a city in the dead of night. Sleepy-eyed linkboys carried their torches through narrow wynds. A priestess sang a call to prayer. Cypress trees swayed gently. She walked along avenues as broad as a river. This was a good place, she was sure of it.

Then a horrible, guttural word shattered the city's calm. And a dread, cobalt light bloomed in the east. Pillars of blue flame taller than redwood trees swept through the city, roaring and whipping up caustic winds. She could almost feel the heat. Screams echoed against high adobe walls, then fell silent. *Run*, she thought, but the pillars swept past her, leaving her unharmed.

She found herself in a courtyard painted with frescoes which blistered then ran from the walls to pool on the floor.

A slender youth, crowned by curls, face frozen in horror, dropped a silver dish of citrus fruits. She heard a single word, *N'chala*, it echoed through her head in a tenor. The youth's lips hadn't moved. He reached towards Dion, but when she outstretched her own hand, he crumbled into ash that was blown away by the winds.

Dion sat bolt upright in bed, covered in a sticky sheen of sweat. She sobbed into her hands, waking Aya, who cradled her, covered her face with kisses, and held her until she slipped back down into dark dreamless sleep.

THE SKY WAS clear and mild on the day the Beaucourt was set to arrive. The women and girls in the dryhouse bustled. Fires burned brighter. Voices louder. Laughs a little too shrill. Dion felt no tingles as she waded out from shore, but Mama Gwe told her that the batch from two days before was shaping up to be something, and her heart felt light. No salt-dreams the night before, and the end of season warmth suffused her limbs, making her feel lithe.

The sun was high in the sky when Kya came running to meet Dion in the shallows. "Beaucourt coming!"

Dion made no special haste, dumped her buckets as usual, then ducked into the dryhouse. Mama Gwe was waiting inside with six boxes of salt, ranging in color from cloud pale to robin egg. Dion nodded.

Trundling down the road at a deceptive speed was the Beaucourt's conveyance, black and silver and gold. In relief against the marsh and the redwoods beyond. It was pulled by a team of four creatures that only resembled horses if you didn't look at them too closely. Mottled grey and black, with manes made of dark, translucent tendrils that moved independently of the wind. Paws instead of hooves.

They seemed to glide effortlessly like cats. No coachman to drive the beasts. The conveyance slowed to a stop just short of the open double doors of the dryhouse. At this distance, its elaborate finery was made clear. It was an ornate six-wheeled carriage decorated with twisting silver filigree vines and heavy ormolu panels. Different, and much richer than the carriage the Beaucourt had travelled in on previous trips to purchase his salt. Dion wondered if this meant a change in his station.

Two gray wraiths slithered out through a panel in the conveyance door. Dion shuddered. The Beaucourt's wraiths moved like octopuses, no fixed shape, undulating through the air as if it was water. They drew open the door, and assisted him to the ground.

The Beaucourt was an ordinary man. Just past middle age. Skin a few shades lighter than the townspeople. Kinky hair combed back from a widow's peak. Kind smile. Judgmental eyes. His robes of office were silver, and unadorned.

Mama Gwe was first to meet him, Dion at her shoulder. Mama Gwe bowed deeply. "It has been too long, old friend. Can I offer you some cool water? Fresh cornbread? Sea greens with trotters?"

The Beaucourt shook his head. "I live in service to the Spiral Senate. The work proceeds. Water will be sufficient."

Mama Gwe gestured. One of the kit-girls brought the Beacourt water in a porcelain cup. He drank it in one pull. He raised an eyebrow. "You have something to show me?"

Mama Gwe had the runners bring out the boxes of salt. The Beaucourt looked them over. His smile grew thin. "It will suffice. But I had hoped the season would be kinder to you."

"Lighter than you want, I reckon. But this ain't all. Dion's our best harvester, and she's prepared a surprise," Mama Gwe said.

Dion climbed the ladder to the second floor, where her salt rested in a refining box. It had time left before it was ready, but it was already the deepest blue she had ever seen. She brought this down for the Beaucourt to view.

A look of undisguised delight crossed his face. "This is excellent! When will it be ready?"

"Needs another fortnight's drying, and then maybe another moon before it's seasoned?" Dion said.

The Beaucourt stroked his chin. "I'll need to make another trip, but this is worth it." He gestured at one of the wraith things. It produced a fat purse of silver and dropped it into Mama Gwe's hands with a shadowy tendril. "Consider this an advance. And if the end results are what this promises, much more will come your way."

The wraiths gathered up the boxes of salt and folded them into themselves. As they swept out after the Beaucourt, one of their trailing tendrils brushed against Dion's cheek. In her head she heard a tenor voice say, "N'chala." In her mind's eye, she saw a youth with curls and a look of quiet desperation.

Dion's cheeks flushed hot with rage. Shame roiled her stomach. She clenched her fists, bent over double and vomited on the floor. She tasted ash. The sweet olu wood smoke smelled like burned flesh. Dion retched again. *This be the ends of our work.* She heard Mama Gwe cry her name, but the call echoed as if across a distance.

The Beaucourt was at her side. He laid a hand on her shoulder. He said a short, sharp word and a feeling of calm invaded her. Her stomach unknotted. He gripped her chin with his other hand. His smile was kind, his eyes judgmental. He sighed. "My dear, you mustn't get too close to my servants. It can be an unpleasant experience for the uninitiated."

Dion was silent through most of dinner. Aya chattered about how best to use their share of the silver, and what to put it towards to make it last. Dion chewed on her chicken bones and sucked the marrow out. Then, without preamble, she said, "The dreams. They happened."

Aya looked up, reverie shattered. "What tells you this?"

"One of the Beacourt's *things*—it passed me by and I knew. It was like, Big Mama once had a salt-dream about one of the Senators being near death and getting healed through the salt. And she knew which one, even though they all wear they masks. *I knew.* Was no hiding it."

"Town relies on the salt. Silver keeps us all afloat, but maybe you ain't got to be the one to harvest it." Aya picked up the coins on the table. "This here will do us, baby."

"That poor boy had his whole life out ahead of him." Dion felt hot, angry tears against her cheek.

"Ain't nothing you can do if it's past." Aya put her hands on Dion's shoulders.

Dion stared into the hearth fire.

Dion ran to the dryhouse in the darkest part of the night. Moon and stars veiled over by the heavy rain clouds that signalled the end of the season. The sea below black ink luminous and glittering with fine-boned fish. Barefoot, she skidded once on the mud-slick path, found her footing and sprinted down to the sandy shore.

The season was over, and the dryhouse was empty. Come morning the girls would expect to turn their hands to preparation and storage, then perhaps take to weaving and hunting until the rain stopped. Dion flung open both doors. The creak was bone-deep and ominous.

Finding by feel and memory the first two porcelain pans, still warm from the day's evaporation, Dion clapped them together and a shuddering *KRACK* rumbled as they met and shattered along invisible fault lines. Great sharp shards clattered to the ground, one wheeling into her leg and nicking her along the thigh. Groping in the darkness, she found the rest of the pans resting on their racks, she hurled them, two, three, four, onto the ground, joy rising in her chest as much as dread at each splintering smash. She stifled a wild high giggle when the eighth and last cracked.

The moon broke through the clouds then, piercing the darkness with its pale light. Blood trickled down Dion's thigh, plashing between her toes. She grabbed a pair of iron tongs and turned over the coals in the firepits. Embers still stirred. She wadded up the linens, but they were still damp from use, and might smother the fire. *The oiled tarps.* They kept the sifters covered and clean of rust. She pulled them off, flung them into the pits, and in moments, heavy smoke roiled up. She overturned a bin of olu wood into the pit. Orange light licked up hungrily to meet the wood. She climbed the ladder up to the refiners. Kicked over boxes of salt. There, still blue as poison, was the last box of lapis salt. This she cradled, and pressed to her chest, aware of all its value and its worth to the town. She climbed down the ladder. Covered her face against the smoke and rushed out into the cool night air. The fire had caught, and it would not be long until someone in the town noticed and tried to rescue the dryhouse. It was too late. Dion walked to the water's edge and stared down at the salt. *The coin from this could salvage everything you love.* She took a long, hard look, and then pitched the box into the sea. The salt was reclaimed by the waters.

Her back to the blaze, Dion knelt in the sand and waited for the tide to come in.

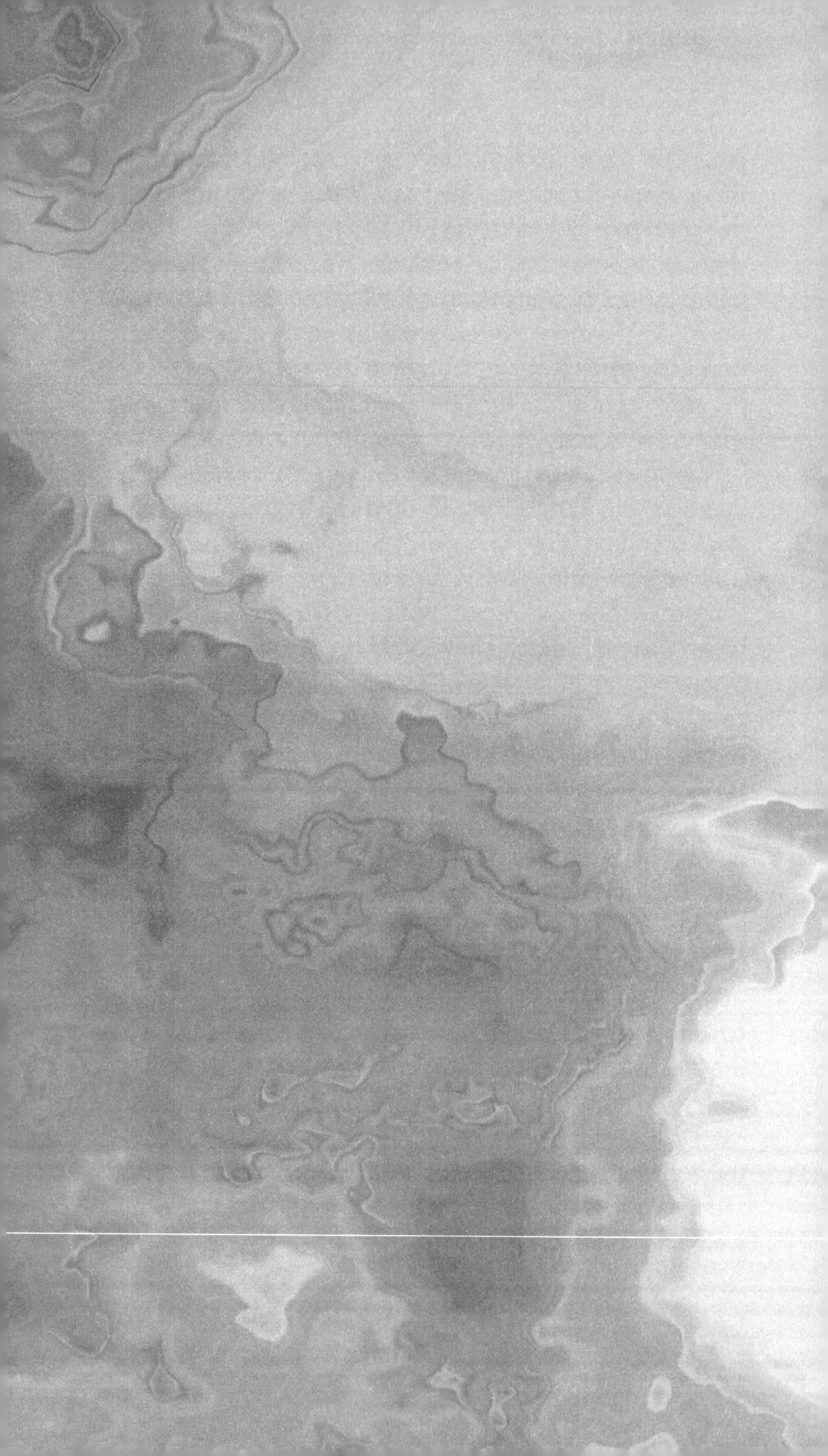

Response

The Calcified Heart of Saint Ignace Battise

O N A THURSDAY night in Harvestmonth, when the moon rises round and bronze as a new betrothal promise watch, is the warlike thrice-veiled Mother of Mákhesthaines, crowned in her black silk mantles embroidered with skulls, permitted across the Holy Square and into the Grand Cathedral of Saint Ignace Battiste.

All other times is she anathema.

The conjunction of astrological events makes this
moonlit night a rare event. Even so, it is often enough
that a grandhomme in xher dotage can witness the most
dedicated foe of our faith—the murderers' patron, the
undying vengeance, the very adversary *herself*—cross the
gates of the Lightcarrier's second holiest city and enter the
Promised-and-Faithful's most hallowed space a handful of
times in one life before xher celestial watch can no longer
be wound.

The terms of the covenant between the Mother of
Mákhesthaines—who slakes her thirst with souls—and
the ancient Parents of the Faith remain unrecorded in
sacred texts. But the results of these accords, forged in
time immemorial, have been seen by denizens of the city
enough that their rituals and circumstance are well-
known to all.

The Mother arrives on foot. She is small and slight,
and hidden beneath her veils, mantles, and gowns of black
byssus—the art of their construction lost when fabled
Seabride was swallowed by the sea. Her step is light, and
though her trains drag behind her, the city's accreted dust
does not stir in her wake.

She is ever accompanied by her two brides. La'acroix,
with long black hair bound up in a tignon of red satin and
jade. She wears a gown of tulle and organza and emerald
brocade. An easy smile, swaying hips, and a gilded
dagger on her throat. Her skin is oiled and gleams in the
bronze moonlight. And bare-breasted Kravat. Tall. Red
hair in plaits. Arms corded with muscle and shoulders
broad enough to yoke. She wears hempen trousers dyed
with woad, and a thin-hammered makhaira on her hips.
If she smiles, it is a thing as sharp as her blade. The
dreaded three then proceed to the Holy Square, which
is at this time empty of all but those who have accepted
Lightcarrier oaths.

The doors of the city basilica stand open before her stalwart enemies. Cathedral linkboys escort them in solemn silence down through the shadowed recesses and vaults of the cathedral to a chapel with an oakblood door. The Mother kneels and enters. Her brides stand beyond the threshold with heads bowed. From a purse beaded with faience, the Mother pulls a key and draws from a monstrance of rose quartz and gold the calcified heart of the blessed city's martyr, Saint Ignace Battiste. In procession as before, they ascend from the cathedral flanked by linkboys. They pass through the funeral arch and cross the bridge of sorrows, where to them the gilded gates of Necropolis are unbarred, and they proceed alone. What happens beyond was unknown.

Until I broke the covenant.

On that strange and sorrowful night when the beaten bronze of the moon broke through the clouds and its terrible aspect cast shadows of the city's spires like the fingers of a skeleton all across the sacred square, I was in attendance, an acolyte. The second cathedral linkboy of two given the duty to escort the mournful Mother to the ebon gates of Necropolis.

After the gates were barred, we were to return to lone cells—the only decoration the symbols of our order: the watch, the swallow, and unburnt heart engraved on bare stone floor—and await in solemn contemplation of our vows until the moon begins its descent. A silent sibling stood sentinel outside our bare cell doors, xher watchful gaze just beyond to remind us of our duty should we falter and attempt egress before the appointed time. But the smallest flaw in this well-appointed, wise reminder to duty is that in our sacred contemplations, we lowly acolytes were tasked to observe the moon's descent. For this purpose were we given a slender arrow slit to gaze upon the sky.

I, a slim and callow youth, given more to curiosity than calm contemplation, stripped off my vestments and silver thread soutane. And sky-clad, slipped through narrow window-slit into the starless night.

Every child in the city and the parishes beyond knows the story of Saint Ignace, martyr-patron of the burned but unharmed heart. How the wretched Mother smote him, spitting venom from her lips! How the wicked brides assailed him with blade, and teeth, and claw! And he alone stood steadfast against them until the coming of the dawn! Undefeated as morn's first rays crested high Necropolis's hill, the wretched Mother's machinations brought to ruin by his undaunted heart. And how she, in her vexation at the city's uncorrupted state, through some infernal power, set noble Ignace all aflame! His tortured cries rose up to heaven. In silence, was she gone. And the city criators, though unworthy, found his ashes where he fell. His body burnt.

But then the golden throated swallows in their millions did descend, and with swift unfaltering wingbeats whirled those ashes in the air to reveal his unburnt heart and his bronzed watch as well! As untarnished as the morning that now spilled over weeping city criators. His promise, then. To still defend us against the evils and our perils. Thus the symbols of our order, the steadfast watch, the heart, the bird.

Think you then what terrors I envisioned, what depredations the sacred relic would endure at the vengeful Mother's hands, as I secretly ascended Necropolis's high hill through its ancient wood.

My eyes were sharp. And long before the order called me to take my vows and serve, I lived a slipthief life, slinking now and then across the city's slate and tiled roofs to do some mischief, when heavy cloud veiled the firmament. I needed no light. But to my astonishment as I crept forward low over root and underbrush, the trees were now illuminated by dancing lights all lapis-colored, no bigger than a pinprick. The source? Docile worms suspended aloft and tied to the tree branches by webs of their own devising, on which dewdrops like glassy pendants caught their mournful light and scattered it across the grounds, casting shadows that shifted as if the trees themselves were set a-sway to the merest breath of wind. And the branches of those trees creaked under the weight of birds! Not only the yellow-throated swallows that long have made their nests in high Necropolis, but resting flush in pairs, uncountable starlings, whose breast plumage was lit with scattering of blue as the lights washed over them, in imitation of the whirling heavens above, concealed from us by clouds. Thus astonished, though sure-foot, I found myself entangled in a sly knot of root and fell forward, my left foot slipping into a place where the rains had collected at the base of a damson plum tree. The dense smell of the earth rose around me, as if it prepared itself for planting. The birds stirred, and then settled. Ahead the trees thinned, and I could see the winding path to the height where the cemetery rotunda stood. Near to the ground, I followed, slipping now and then behind a crypt, a tangle of brambles full to bursting with blackberries, or cracked tombstone. The three continued their accession undeterred: doe-eyed La'acroix first, swaying to music known only to her, grim Kravat at the rear, hand resting on the hilt of her blade. Between them, the Mother of Mákhesthaines, carrying Saint Ignace's stonelike heart on a cushion of cloth-of-gold next to her bosom where no heart could beat. They passed near enough to me that I could hear the whisper of the Mother's byssus-gowns. Their scents, attar of roses, sweat, and ancient spices mingled into one.

They came then to the heights of Necropolis, where stood the cemetery rotunda. There rest the bones and remnants of all the city criators, and the lesser saints and martyrs.

On its dome stands a statue of Saint Ignace Battiste struck in bronze by Clerval Grandeure himself. Arm outstretched with steadfast watch and his own heart carried in one hand just beneath the place that heart should sit. His features sweet. Serene. And for three hundred paces all around the rotunda's prominence the grounds were cleared of trees and underbrush. This space was bare of all else excepting other smaller monuments, sweet grass, and heavy flagstones. Among these monuments I made my way behind the devilish three to uncover for myself what cruel, unnatural torments they planned for that noble sacred heart.

They ventured not to the rotunda. An unadorned plinth, chest-height to me—even at that youthful age—stood weathered and alone at the top, shadowed over by rotunda. And the Mother made her way to this. Her brides removed all her mantles with reverence and laid them down on the flagstones beneath. With ceremony and care, La'acroix and Kravat moved as one and took from the Mother of Mákhesthaines's gloved hands the sacred heart resting on its golden cushion. Their movements were deft, and they carried the heart to sit atop the plinth as if it would shatter from the merest bump. The mother shrugged out of the first of her byssus-gowns. She wore on her bosom an ancient bronze promise watch fastened to her by chains of gold, which her brides then unwrapped. The moon caught her then, and from behind a marble bust of Saint Calave I saw her face: youthful, large eyes, a strange color that northerners sometimes have, like the winter sea. Her lips were full, and her brow unlined. A black curl of hair tumbled down from her pinned locks and nestled against her cheek. The adversary herself looked barely more than a girl. Unchained from the watch she cradled—whose burnished bronze and uncracked enamel made it the very replica of the great relic of our order—she placed it with all solemnity on the plinth, next to the stony heart of slain Saint Ignace. Her brides turned their backs to her and lowered their heads.

For a moment all was in perfect silence. The moon cast away the shadow of the rotunda and limned the Mother, the brides, and the plinth in its light. I scarce dared breathe. And then? Saint Ignace's heart began to beat! Not some trick of the light! In the quiet I could hear it echo across the bald apex of Necropolis's high hill. In perfect time with the Mother's own promise watch. From behind me and all around came the cry of the yellow-throated swallows, and the starlings rose up in murmuration, black against white cloud. The swallows themselves flew low over the hill—I felt the beat of their wings as they passed—and wreathed the beating heart, the watch, and the plinth. Sometime do birds aflight take the semblance of strange things, but these clustered ever tighter and gave the figure of a man. I saw sinew then, and fingers, not passing suggestions from a moment's angle in a far-off living smoke. Then feathers rained down before the Mother, and the figure *was* a man. Naked, sat upon the plinth, a face carved on effigy and coin, only now rendered mortal. No more beautiful than mine. It was the blessed saint, I was sure of it. His hair as kinked and coiled as my own. His nose broad, and forehead creased by worry, not the placid beaming icon, nor the open-handed martyr of mosaic scenes. A man, handsome, but no more remarkable than any dark-skinned crafter from the city's artificieries. He had a glazier's scar upon his shoulder. He looked only at the Mother, and the scorn and worry fell away to something tender.

She took his chin in her hand. "And you return to me once more?"

The moon vanished behind a cloud, and yet, I could see tears upon his cheek. "Nothing can keep me from it. I will return to you always. Always. Always."

Her brides clothed him in her own mantles. The Mother's voice was soft, and though the night still and I three arm's lengths away, I did not hear her reply.

The saint spoke in a firmer timbre. "You should have razed all their works. And left the ground scoured of life." His mouth was firm.

The Mother of Mákhesthaines said, "No. For vengeance sake, I could bathe in all their blood and remain dry. But whilst their enchantment persists, we can be together for a night when the moon renews our promise."

"It is fleeting for you," said the saint.

"And one night is how one begins a life. I will have my lifetime of them."

A taste, both sweet and foul, rose from my throat to my lips. I spit in the crook of my arm. These things we believed true: the violation, the sacrifice serene, the city's salvation—the very bedrock of our faith—were all false. I had sworn myself over to invention as false as my own oath.

Did you think I gasped at the discovery? Or, in momentary shock, stepped backwards onto a wayward twig, drawing the ire of the blessed saint down upon me? Or that I scrabbled nude down the hillside on all fours chased by limbless horrors conjured by the Mother of Mákhesthaines's poisoned breath? No, those are such tales a parrain frightens his goodchildren to obedience with around the hearth. I wiped my sick on the bark of a tree, wincing a little at its roughness and crept away unobserved by Mother, brides, and saint. I left their tender ministrations undisturbed. I returned to my cell to await the dawn with little more than a scratch and a muddy left foot.

But the next morning, I and my fellow watcher linkboy were tasked with inspecting all the relics from nave to altar. From Saint Calave's reliquary to Saint Ignace's untarnished watch that betrothed used to keep their time and pilgrims pray towards for healing light. I followed close behind the prioress, who unveiled the great relic, the Faithful-and-Promised watch. It has run without winding since before the cathedral's first-placed arch and remained untarnished as the day the fires brought it from beneath

Saint Ignace's robes into the dawn. Its time was true. But as I brushed and oiled its surface, just there, beneath the crown was a single spot of verdigris. As if from above a single salty tear fell on that peerless device. The prioress pulled a clean cloth from beneath her soutane and wiped the spot until it shone again. Almost new.

Did I think to leave the Order? Declaim to Light-Seated Ductrix all its lies? What would happen to the city then, its pieties all undone? Would the charms that ever preserved us founder with the truth? The city that was all my world and whose streets and citizens I loved as much as vengeful witch ever loved wronged saint, could I bear to bring its doom? And I had witnessed miracles, and when you have witnessed miracles the taste for heresy is cold. In short: I was a coward, and turned myself more devoutly to my oaths, even knowing their mettle was ridden with rot and decay. I served, and rose through the ranks.

A score of years passed until the confluence of the heavens led again to the rising of that bronze and awful moon. I was by then chapel monsignor and blessed the new-chose linkboys, who knelt beneath the watch to pray, unveiled for that sacred purpose. It shone as if burnished. I, alone, watched its face. The count of its smallest hand was slow, and for that briefest moment, so was my own heart. But the Mother came as always, and night passed to morning as it must.

Another three-and-twenty years. I had occasion to inspect the oakblood door and prepare the vault beyond for cleansing. Beneath its monstrance, was that dust or signs the heart itself had at long last, began to crumble under the impossible weight it carried? But at the dawn returned the Mother with her brides still in tow.

The Grand Abbot perished from consumption after thirteen years' long fight. And in the waning years remaining me, I attend the Archlamplighter herself.

Tonight, again, rises that moon! Three days prior an envoy from the far-off Spiral Senate has arrived, his Beaucourt close at hand, reeking of foul magics. And the Queendom has withdrawn its protecting armies from its outward marches, where the city still remains. The sorcerers of the Chant Real in gleaming Sarraclay have failed their glamour-casting, and the queen is ill-at-ease. The air smells of smoke and of blood. I think now on the saint, and the adversary's reply *whilst their enchantment persists*. Does that high-esteemed watch tarnish still? Does that heart's stone remain as hard? Will the Mother and the brides stand atop high Necropolis's hill and reunite once more? Does he come? I search the darkening heavens for swallows and their golden throats, else the starling numbers descending down like feathered smoke. But my eyes are old. And does he come? What means *always* to the dead?

Deep Like the Rivers

I LOVED MY BOY, but I never understood him. Momma would have. They would have taken to each other like bees and flowers. Sometimes it felt like her old eyes were staring out of his little face. He'd make me so mad. That calm. Insisting he knew so much I didn't. Insisting he knew things he had no right to know.

When I was a little girl, momma told me if I ever lost someone I loved to write his name in red ink seven times on a piece of onionskin paper. Wrap the paper around John the Conquer root and a rock as big as my fist. Tie the whole thing up with a bright red ribbon, then bury it in the sand. Low tide under the next full moon.

If I found that ribbon-wrapped rock after seven days and seven nights, the lost one would come back to me. I found out too late that the sea takes all things.

Momma was what they called back home a root-worker. Used to say she could *conjure*. When I was seven, angry at the boys who chased me across the playground and threw my books on the cafeteria roof, angry at the white teachers for not caring, angry that I didn't have soft yellow hair, I came in to Momma's kitchen. I slammed her screen door, tracked in dirt from the outside. And she must have known, because she didn't scold. Her hands didn't stop moving. She continued chopping garlic for the big pot of red beans simmering on the stove.

"So?" She said, the question cut off by a chop.

"It's not fair. It's NOT fair. When am I gonna get power like you to make bad people stop hurting me?"

She clattered the knife down on the chopping board. She swept me in her arms. She smelled like starch and onions and pound cake batter. "Baby, it don't work like that. It ain't in the *blood*. It chooses who it chooses. And ain't nothing can stop not one of us from being hurt."

"Then what good is it?" I wailed.

"I can teach you to set a bone with a kind word and cool water. To keep an enemy from your door with graveyard dust. To bring back home a lost loved one. To sing to rest a heart full of grief. But can't nobody stop you from being hurt. Not while you're living."

"Teach me, Momma. I want to learn."

She slid me to the floor, gentle. She smoothed the flyaways from my pigtails. "You go along and do your homework first. Then we'll eat supper." She rested her hands on her hips for a moment then turned back to chopping her garlic. I sniffled.

"And then *maybe* we have a little time for you to learn what I know."

Momma was a good teacher, patient and exact. I was a bad student.

WHEN ISAIAH WAS five, his teacher, a nervous white woman with oversized glasses and Lucille Ball red hair suggested to me and Roderick that maybe he should be held back in school another year. "I have concerns that little Izzy isn't able to keep up with the rest of the class." She pressed her thin lips into a smile. "Particularly in reading."

"Excuse me, Ms. Cowan?" I used my business voice. "*Isaiah* has been reading since he was three."

"We've had him tested—" Roderick said.

That thin smile again. "Mrs. Daubert," she pronounced it *dob-bert*, "I know every parent wants to believe their child is exceptional, but—"

"As my husband was saying, we've had Isaiah tested by a psychologist, and there's nothing wrong with his intellectual development." I scooted upright in the metal folding chair. "The psychologist did suggest that sometimes *bright* children can be bored by rote exercises."

I took a mean bit of pleasure in her expression.

That night, we took Isaiah out to McDonald's. He ignored the toy that came with his happy meal and drew pictures on the border of a napkin. Tiny precise figures in blue and green. Women with shark fins and hair billowing up like kelp. Men with twisted mouths and eyes on the same side of their face, like flounders.

"Your teacher says you're not paying attention in class when they do reading," I said.

"I can read." Isaiah said, not looking up from his drawing.

"Buddy," Rod said mouth half-full of fries. "Sometimes you have to do stuff you already know how to. It seems silly, but it'll help you be what you want to be when you grow up."

"I want to be a mermaid when I grow up." His face was fierce, solemn.

Rod laughed. "Scooter, you're a boy. Boys can't be mermaids."

"I can *too* be a mermaid." Isaiah colored in a figure with a foam green crayon. "I can be anything."

BY THE TIME Isaiah was twelve, I figured out he was what Momma would have called "sweet." Rod would have had a problem with that, if he could have bothered with being around. But Isaiah was still just my boy. My smart, serious little boy.

One Saturday I was doing laundry and was in his warren of a room looking for whites when I came across a spiral notebook wedged between his headboard and the wall. I opened it, thinking I'd find drawings of Atlantis. Instead there were drawings of other boys in impossible sexual positions. The name Jason written on three different pages with hearts around it. My heart sunk. The world was already hard enough for a little black boy who would be seen as nothing more than a nigger. Now he'd be seen as a faggot too.

When Isaiah came home from music practice, I was waiting in the living room with the notebook on my lap. He bounced in carrying his violin case in one hand and a sheaf of music in another. "Mom, you'll never guess what—" He trailed off when he saw the notebook.

"Isaiah, honey. I found this in your room. We have to talk about this."

"Mom. Those were my things. They were private things." He stared at the wall, blinking back tears.

"There's no privacy when you're living under my roof, you hear!" My face felt hot. I remembered the betrayal I felt when Momma read through my diary and found out I kissed a Bobby Jenkins from down the street. *Not gonna be with them no 'count Jenkins.*

His voice was raised, not quite a shout. "You had *no* right. You had no *right*."

I don't know why I didn't take him to my chest. Didn't stroke his hair and tell him things will be fine. I had to protect him, didn't I? How could I protect him if he hid things from me? "I think you forgot who here is the parent. You don't use that tone with me. You go to your room until you can talk to me right."

The look he gave me was his father's, measured and cold. I loved my child, but I wanted to slap him across the mouth just then. He said quietly, "Yes, ma'am."

There was a tightness to his walk, a way of squaring his shoulders that brought out the spite in me. "And don't think you can slam my doors. You don't pay any bills around here!"

The deliberate care with which he shut that door was his silent rebuke.

HE TOOK UP surfing. It started with boogie boards, but as he grew more confident on the water, he asked for a surfboard. Things were tight, but I'd saved up for driving lessons for him and he showed no interest in driving. I got him that surfboard for his sixteenth birthday. He was growing up. Dark like his father, and already taller. He had my suspicious mouth and Momma's old, weary eyes. I used to drop him off in Malibu for surfing lessons and pick him up after. Uncle Freeland had left me his big ugly Buick station wagon in his will, and we put a rack on top for the surfboard.

One of those hot and cloudy Southern California days when the air feels heavy, I decided I'd stay out on the beach while he surfed.

"I was thinking that today I might get my ankles wet and lay out on the sand instead of heading up to IHOP."

Isaiah didn't look at me. "Okay."

"You're not embarrassed by your old mother, are you? I'll wear a floppy hat and those big sunglasses and you can pretend you don't know me."

He kissed me on the cheek. Quick. Hard. "I love you, little ma. Of course I'm not embarrassed."

The drive out was quieter than usual. He made a comment that the chaparral reminded him of seaweed as we drove through Laurel Canyon. I rolled down my window. An old smell of woodsmoke. The salt tang of the ocean we could not see.

I watched my boy out on the waves. He seemed so confident and loud and carefree. He was different on the water. After his lessons he splashed around with some of the other boys until they drifted away into whirls and knots of two or three.

I saw him talking to the only other black boy on the beach. High yellow and pretty, this strange boy rested his naked chest against a rocky outcrop. He kept his legs under the water. It was overcast, but that boy's skin shimmered. This boy looked at my son like he was something good to eat. My boy looked back at him the same. My palms itched. I wanted to pull my boy by the ear away from him. I turned my attention back to my true crime novel.

I got so engrossed at how some white man killed his wife and almost got away with it that I didn't hear Isaiah tromp back across the sand. His lanky shadow striped my torso. I looked up from my book. "Who's your friend?"

He ignored the question. "Ma, did you know all the waters in the world are connected?"

I looked over at the outcrop. The pretty boy was no longer there. "I did not know that." I rose to my feet, pulled my beach towel up.

"Well they are, and I don't just mean how lakes go into streams that go into rivers that go into the sea. They're all really the same thing. I feel like I'm touching the world when I'm out there on the waves." His smile was unguarded. My heart hurt a little. I knew how rare those little boy smiles were.

"Hey, you know when you were little you told your dad you wanted to be a mermaid when you grew up? And he said—"

The smile faded, like a cloud crossing over the sun. "I remember."

We both stood there looking out at the rocky outcrop and the waters beyond it.

HE STARTED STAYING out late. Strange men would call the house. His grades got worse. He wouldn't tell me where he was going. One night he came home soaking wet, smelling like the ocean, with hickeys all along his neck. The Perry Ellis pullover he'd worn out was gone.

I roared at him. "You still are under my roof. You think you're grown? Where have you been, Isaiah Baptiste Daubert?"

He smirked. His voice cracked into song. "If you go out on the sea today you're sure of a big surprise. If you go out on the waves today—" he spun in a circle and pointed at me. "—*you* better go in disguise. For every fish that ever was will gather there for certain because today's the day the mermaids have their picnic."

I grabbed him by the wrist. His skin was slippery and cool. "Have you been drinking? What do you think you're doing?"

"Only the nectar of the deep. And I think I'm falling in love."

I'd never raised my hand to my boy. I'd wanted to, but I'd never done it. I slapped him. "You will not disrespect me or my house."

"My father's house has many rooms." He reeled back. He steadied himself on a kitchen chair. "Most of them are sunken."

Momma would have known what to do. She would have seen what was happening. Momma would have given him a broth stinking of sage. Would have slipped the right ribbon under his pillow. Would have whispered a charm. *I* slapped him again. "What you are not going to do is go out with strange men and come home stinking of seawater and drink. You are not going to have whoring ways and nasty manners. I am not breaking my back working for you to do whatever the hell you want."

His shoulders sagged. He crouched down so we were the same height. "I'm sorry Ma. Let's not fight. I'll take a shower and we can watch *The Five Heartbeats*."

His breath smelled like rotting kelp and raw fish. My stomach turned. "Go to your room. I don't want to see you again."

I meant to say I don't want to see you again *tonight*.

THEY TOLD ME he drowned. Nice Latino policeman and his blonde partner who looked at me like she smelled something nasty. There was no body. They found his board cracked in two, floating on the waves. Found his board shorts on the sand.

"Those shorts were shredded, ma'am," the blonde said. "Probably caught on a rock, or maybe some sort of sea animal—"

Her partner nudged her. "Mrs. Daubert? I know this must come as a terrible shock. I'm afraid I have to ask you a few questions."

"It's Baptiste, actually. Hasn't been Daubert since the divorce. Do you mind if I sit?" Before waiting for an answer, I sunk into the blue and white la-z-boy that was Isaiah's favorite seat. It smelled faintly like him. "He is... was...*is* an excellent swimmer, Officer."

He looked sheepish. "We're not going to stop looking, but I need you to know in cases like this, the outcome is most often not the best."

I SOLD MOST of my things except for Uncle Freeland's Buick. I sold the little bungalow where I'd lived for 15 years. I moved back home to Louisiana with my sister. Couldn't stand to be anywhere near the Pacific. After we had the funeral with its empty casket, Rod kept calling me until I blocked his number. He wasn't there for Isaiah when he was here, no point in him trying to be a father after my boy was gone.

Two grey years passed. Each day ate a little into my savings. My sister kept trying to get me to do something, anything but miss Isaiah. First good-naturedly, then cajoling, finally exasperated. I decided to clear out the crawlspace. Momma had left all sorts of debris up there.

I was crouched over and aching from pulling out cardboard boxes with old report cards and yellowed newspapers when I found a little notebook. It used to be red, but was so covered in dust and cobwebs that it was now the brown of old photographs. I opened it. In fading ink in my own shaky childish hand I'd written, "How to bring back lost love."

There was still some Great John De Conquer root in the back yard. And red ribbon couldn't possibly be difficult to obtain. I thought to myself *why not?*

ON THE SEVENTH night of the seventh day I drove myself down to the river in the Buick. I took a good strong flashlight. I knew I was in the exact place I'd buried that rock. I shone my light across the mud. There was a hole a little bigger than my fist near the gnarled cottonwood root I'd used as a marker.

A wind blew across the water and showered me with cottonwood fluff. In one of the tree's branches I caught a glimpse of a swallow-like bird with shiny black feathers. It had something red in its beak, like a ribbon. I set to with my spade, stabbing at the mud, plunging my hands in and feeling for rocks. Knowing all the while that the hole I'd left it in was empty. I kept at it until my hands cracked and bled. Until I was out of breath. Then I leaned against the cottonwood and wept.

The surface of the river looked greasy under the moonlight. I heard Isaiah's voice clear in my mind, "All the waters of the world are connected."

I wiped the snot from my face with the least muddy part of my sleeve. I walked back up the bank to Uncle Freeland's Buick and sat behind the wheel. Thought about all the times I should have listened more. Should have been more patient. I thought of how I should have just watched the Five fucking Heartbeats. Then I gunned it.

The Buick loped down the riverbank, slipping in the mud, losing traction but not getting stuck. The splash as I reached the water was horrendous, and I thought it just might crack the windshield. The river was fast and deep, and the Buick and I sank like a ribbon-wrapped stone.

THE HEADLIGHTS LIT the murk outside the Buick, but the headlights gave out all too soon. I'd left my flashlight in the mud. In the dark the Buick and I kept falling, and I couldn't tell if I had hit the bottom. I was suspended upside down in my seatbelt. I heard the glass crack, then a cold spray of dank river water hit me in the face. Great glugs escaped the car, and I knew it would soon be filled with the river. I groped in the dark for the steering wheel and pulled my head up as far as I could. "Please," I shouted. "I just want to see Isaiah one last time. I need to tell him I'm sorry."

The glass cracked again, and this time the water flooded the car. I took one last panicked breath, and then reached up to unlatch my seatbelt. It was stuck.

I hung there for a moment in the dark and cold, trying not to scream, my lungs already pounding. A ghostly blue light filled the car's interior. Was I going to heaven? The light grew stronger, and I counted the seconds before I would have to gasp again, and then swallow river water and silt.

I could make out a figure. The boy from the shore. He was the blue light. Rather than legs he had a long flat fluked tail, like a dolphin. The light radiated out from his shimmery skin, green now under the murk instead of golden. He opened his mouth and rows of small, spiny teeth gave out the same light. He swam up close. His eyes were black with pinpoint pupils. He reached out a long-fingered hand and I saw webs between those fingers. He grabbed my throat. Clutched it tight. I screamed, thinking I was going to be choked, then noticed I could breathe.

The sea creature spoke. "You can't stay here."

I looked at him. Only I was no longer sure the creature was a *him*. *They* shimmered iridescently, and their form seemed in flux. One moment his face was square and masculine, and another it seemed that small tender breasts budded from her chest, and her gaze was girlish and tender.

What I thought were dolphin flukes suddenly expanded out to octopus arms with gripping suckers, and then collapsed into long, human like legs. I looked into their face, into shark eyes fringed with thick black eyelashes, and said without accusation, "You took my son."

They shook their head. "No. Isaiah chose to come with me. Willingly and of his own accord. It *has* to be that way."

"I drove him away."

The mermaid, and I believed that I now understood what mermaids really were, stroked my cheek. "No. A part of him always belonged to the sea."

"Can I talk to him?"

"There isn't much time. My power to keep you breathing won't last."

"I need to say goodbye."

The mermaid smiled. Those terrible sharp teeth with their blue glow shone between pouty lips. He grabbed onto my wrist. "I can give you that."

A warmer current buffeted me. Threatened to tear me away, but the mermaid's grip was strong and he stayed with me. Another blue glow, weaker this time, from behind me. I turned. Isaiah was there. He was changed. His fingers were longer, webs between them, his legs ended in flippers instead of feet. He smiled at me. His teeth were still human but had already begun to glow blue.

"Little Ma!" He gave me a look like he'd woken up on Christmas morning. He furrowed his brow, jutted out his jaw. He looked a wild thing. "I tried to tell you. I knew Daddy wouldn't get it, but I thought you—I *told* you I could be a mermaid!" He bit his lower lip. Then squeezed his eyes shut. When he opened them, the wildness in them was calmed. "You shouldn't look so sad."

I pounded my fists against his chest. "I thought you were dead!"

He held my fists in one hand—when did he get so strong? Then leaned forward to kiss my cheek. "I don't believe Grandma Lou never told you about us people."

I looked at my boy and the mermaid. "I never believed."

"You found me. You must have believed some." Another unguarded smile.

I began to weep, my tears warm on my cheeks. "I wanted to say I'm sorry. I wanted to say you deserved better as a mother. I wanted to say that I love you and—"

Isaiah embraced me. His skin felt rubbery and cool. "Ma? Mommy. You did the best you could. You were the best mother you knew how to be. I'm grateful for all you've done for me."

"Are you safe?"

The mermaid moved closer to my son. "There isn't much time, beloved. Say your farewells."

"Safe? Ma, there isn't any safe on the land, or under it. I'm not safe. But I'm happy." He let go of my hands. He did look happy.

I said, "I love you."

The water churned and swirled and I rocketed upwards. The blue lights shrank away into pinpoints. The water which I had been inhaling without thinking turned thick in my nose and mouth. I broke through the surface, coughed and sputtered for a moment. The moon was bright, and all the stars were out. I wasn't a strong swimmer, so I drifted with the current and made my way to shore. Not safe but happy was the best that any black boy could hope for.

Counting Her Petals

NOW

ON A WARM, clear day that smells like pink jasmine, Cleo stands on the front porch of her girlfriend's craftsman bungalow, opens the screen door and knocks three times. She holds the key to the house in her right hand. The jagged edges dig into her palm. Starlings in the big ficus shading the front yard startle upwards, but nothing comes from within. She tries the doorbell again, hears the three tinny electronic bongs one after another, but nothing stirs. She sighs. Aster had given her this key.

For emergencies, Cleo had said. Or if you just want to surprise me in the bath, Aster replied. Cleo unlocks the door and turns the handle. Daylight pours into the front room, casting a long Cleo-shadow across the hardwood floor. Motes of dust dance in the light dappled through the leaves of the ficus. "A-babe?" Cleo calls.

Cleo steps inside. The front room is neat. She can smell the lemony scent of furniture polish just underneath the heady fragrance of pink jasmine that wafts in behind her. She smells no onions or garlic or fried peppers from the kitchen; Aster loves to cook, and never uses a light hand with aromatics or spices. Cleo sometimes teases her about her hands smelling good enough to eat; Aster uses lemon juice and soap to tame down the allium scents, but they cling to her fingers after chopping. Cleo walks into the kitchen. "Aster?" she yells, not expecting an answer. Everything stored properly, nothing in the sink. She opens the fridge. No leftovers. No fresh fruit. Aster always, always makes too much food for one or even two people to eat. Cleo bites her lower lip.

She makes her way to Aster's office, past the master bedroom. Its door is open, the bed made and no clothes laid out for the next day. The office door is closed. Cleo feels apprehensive as she places a hand on the door. "Aster?" she calls. This space is the most private place in the house. She opens the door. Cleo is not a screamer. There is a willfulness to her practiced calm. Nonetheless, she finds herself biting back a shriek at the scene. What comes out is half-swallowed, "No."

Aster lies naked on the floor, tangled up in cables and tubes. Cleo kneels next to her, feels warm breath on her cheek, and reaches for Aster's wrists. She pauses, sees an arterial line snaking out from Aster's right wrist. Above them, monitors display heartrate, blood pressure, and other numbers that Cleo doesn't recognize. An empty IV bag is on its stand, a tube set up for a fluid drip inserted neatly into Aster's left arm; a machine attached to it beeps softly. Aster's skin is dry and cool, slightly ashy. Her lips are chapped. Eyes shut, but Cleo can see Aster's eyeballs dart beneath her eyelids. Tangled in her hair are LED lights and cables glued to her scalp at irregular intervals. The lights display numbers and sigils that Cleo doesn't recognize. Server lights blink. Cleo brushes her hand gently across Aster's cheek. "A-Babe?"

Cleo draws back her hand and slaps Aster sharply across that cheek. An HDMI cable connected somewhere just below Aster's ear jiggles. Eyelids flutter, but no answer. Cleo follows the cable along its path, one of a bank connected to a server near three monitors on a desk with a keyboard.

She places a hand on the server, closes her eyes, and reaches for Aster, holding in her mind Aster's smell, the sound of her laugh, and the tender places at the back of her knee, as a bright minty color. After a moment, Cleo feels the color bloom faintly from the server in response. *There.*

Cleo sighs. She sits on her haunches and listens to Aster's breathing. It is steady. She leaves the room to gather her supplies.

LONG AGO

SHE NEVER START a story with once upon a time. No, she say, "Long ago..."

Well then, long ago there was a little gal with little gal black patent leather shoes. She had dust-brown hair tied in tight pigtails capped by plastic barrettes in the shape of a ribbon. She was best-loved by her mama, her Gramma Augusta, and her Great-Gramma, Dear. Dear lived in a little yellow house with a big garden and it was the place that the little gal with pigtails and a hard head loved best in all the world.

One day Dear give her five dollars to bring back some butter. Now, Dear tell that gal to walk straight to the store and straight back, and tell her she can buy something for herself. The gal walk straight to the corner store and she use her "Yes, please," and "No, thank you, ma'am," in the shop, and the shopkeeper give her an extra pack of Now and Laters for free because the gal has such nice manners. Skipping over the cracks in the sidewalk, the girl sing an old, sweet song. That song tickle her throat, and the sweet red Now and Later tingle her tongue. She had good manners, like a big girl, she think, and just like that, she grow hard-headed. "Come straight home," Great-Gramma Dear told her, but the girl saw an open gate into a yard full of flowers. They smell so sweet, she think she could stop and look for a moment—looking ain't hurt nobody—and she walk right into that garden without a care for what she been told.

THEN

THE SECOND TIME I met you I was working. Sustainability was a buzzword, and the nursery had been contacted by a big nonprofit who wanted the decorations for their benefit gala to be repurposed after the champagne stopped flowing to enrich some underprivileged school's parched asphalt playground. Thing is, the kind of showy florals that look good in a glossy press release ain't always the same kind of plant that survives a dusty shade-starved schoolyard and the curious hands of children. The hibiscus, strelitzia, petunia, and chaparral clematis planted in boxes or carefully draped over trellises wouldn't survive a night of drinking and dancing, much less enrich the lives of inner city kids and their tetherball courts without some personal attention. That attention was me, the "miracle worker."

You were also working. Setting up some kind of complicated digital displays, hiding the wires and electrical tape, and making it look easy. I had seen you a week before on the balcony of Lita's Miracle Mile apartment looking out towards the Hollywood Hills. I'd had three beers, and asked Lita about you. She scoffed and called you "Little Miss Perfect," and I thought you *were*, with your long legs and smooth dark skin—what Mama called "blue-black"—and the hollow at the base of your throat. You were wearing a backless blouse that looked expensive, and even though I was a little tipsy and very *thirsty,* I was too shy to try my game on Little Miss Perfect.

I trundled in a flower box full of purple petunias, and you talked to me. Your voice was low and every word perfectly enunciated. "Such a lovely color," you said.

"They're a kind of nightshade! Relatives of deadly nightshade, but also potatoes, tomatoes, chili peppers..." I trailed off. I was being boring about plants again.

But you smiled at me, and your interest seemed genuine. "Fascinating. You must tell me more—" A question hovered in the air.

"I'm Cleo." I held out a hand. You shook it. Your skin was cool and soft.

"Aster," you said.

"Pretty name! It's also the name of the genus of flowering—"

You laughed. It was like the thrum of a guitar. "I know, I chose it."

NOW

CLEO WATCHES THE rise and fall of Aster's chest for a moment before she begins. No cornmeal in the kitchen, so she has chosen to improvise instead of leave the house. She opens a box of instant grits—the Quaker smiling beatifically from its side—and crouches down to carefully trace out a complicated sigil on the hardwood floor. With her fingers she deftly defines straight lines and sweeps dry grits into circles with the same care she pinches back marigolds. She fights her impatience and sense of urgency and throws herself into the work with care and precision, and the vèvè takes shape. She looks down at the central cross, the curls that radiate out from it, and the four small circles with their own crosses. It is a respectful rendering. She stands, and pours rum into a pair of mugs; one with a cartoon figure smirking, a chipped rim and dark rims where it has been stained by tea, the other a deep-blue with gold specks, handmade by Aster and fired in a kiln just north of Santa Barbara.

She takes a swig from the tea-stained mug. The rum is caramel against her tongue, then licorice, then fire at the back of the throat. Warmth spreads through her chest. She holds up the blue mug and offers it up to the air. Her voice is hoarse and husky. "Papa Legba, open the barrier so that I may pass. Open the barrier to the spirit world so I may pass. Legba, Open the barrier."

Nothing happens. Cleo takes another swig and continues to chant. "Open the barrier so that I may pass to the spirit world. Papa Legba, open the barrier." She feels a prickling at the back of her neck. An itch in her scalp. "Open the barrier so that I may pass. Legba, open the barrier to the spirit world."

The curlicues and lines of the grits-vèvè glow a soft green—the glow-in-the-dark color of children's toys— and the rum in the blue mug begins to roil and froth. There is thunder in Cleo's voice now. "Papa Legba at the crossroads, Papa Legba behind the mirror. Open the barrier to the spirit world so that I may pass!"

Aster keeps the windows in her office closed, but a hot wind heavy with the scent of sumac and cumin whips through them, scattering loose papers and rattling the venetian blinds. Cleo downs the last of the rum in her mug. Streams of vapor from the blue mug waft into the wind. Grits are caught up in a dust devil, but the vèvè keeps its shape and glows a darker green. "Royal Legba, guardian of the gates! I cry out to you, open the barrier, unbar the gates so that I may pass."

An electric hum permeates the room. Cleo can feel its resonance in her bones. The wires and the monitors are limned in a pale blue. *Saint Elmo's fire,* she thinks. She looks down at Aster, recumbent and peaceful in the localized tempest. Cleo clenches her fists. She roars. "Open the barrier!"

The wind howls. The screensaver on the central monitor—a slideshow of Aster's favorite places—is dispelled and Cleo sees an old-fashioned dialogue box with a yellow border appear on the monitor. It has buttons marked *yes* and *no,* and a single sentence written in all caps: *ARE YOU SURE?*

Buffeted by the spicy wind, Cleo crosses over to the keyboard, which glows with that unearthly cold fire. She presses "tab" and then hits enter to mark *yes.*

The wind's whine becomes a howl and the monitor wrinkles and warps, splitting in the middle. The air smells of ozone and burning plastic. Fractal lines radiate outwards from the tear. Auroral reds and oranges dance from in the darkness beyond the gap, which seems to open onto a chasm much deeper than a flatscreen monitor could hide. Cleo reaches one hand towards the widening hole and vanishes.

THEN

YOU COOKED FOR me on our first date. Rice and peas with ackee and saltfish. It was delicious, and I said so. I said I would have to make you my special gumbo.

You said, "That presumes we're going to see each other again."

Ain't gonna lie, I was cocky. I saw the way you looked at my biceps, and I was dressed sharp. "Oh, I bored you already? Girl, you ain't even seen my good tattoos."

"I'll admit, I am curious." Your voice was a purr. "But you've put me all out of ackee."

I smirked. "I got you. With the gumbo. The next time."

You said, "I do like a woman with healthy appetites."

I stood up and stretched. "You can see I ain't been missing too many meals."

We kissed. I put my hand on the back of your neck. Your skin was so soft.

"I ain't got nowhere to be tomorrow," I said.

"I do," you said, "but I think I can live with being late."

Your body was tight and lithe against me, and I wanted to lick that hollow in your throat.

You placed your hands on my hips and gently pushed me away. I was surprised, but figured if you had changed your mind, wasn't nothing I could do.

"You should know that I'm trans," you said.

You were all confidence and coolness before, but there was something fragile in your eyes. I said, "I'm Cleo."

You laughed and told me to shut it and took me to bed.

LONG AGO

THAT GARDEN OWNED by a woman call herself Mother Bea. Say Mother Bea knew magic. From the window she look at that hard-headed brown girl with the pink barrettes and skinned knees play in her garden's forked paths among the hydrangea and the frangipani. She think to herself this little girl could be her own sweet Sarah. She knew a conjure that command the bees. She say a word and they close the garden gate behind them. She say another word and they fly to the four o'clock flowers. They bees tease them open and the smell drift out heavy, like perfume. That nobbin-hearted gal feel dizzy like she been drinking wine. Ol' Mother Bea creep out and say in her goodest, sweetest voice, "You look unwell, my child. Can I get you a cool drink? Maybe a piece of toast and jam?"

Now this gal's gramma Augusta, and her mama, and her great-gramma Dear all been told her not to trust no stranger. But Mother Bea had a kind face and a soft voice, and the gal figure nothing bad could happen so long as she could see the garden gate, so she gone and set down at that woman's table.

And she geta cold drink, and some toast with plenty jam besides. The woman talk to her sweetly, and the gal tell her all about Dear's garden; not as big as Mother Bea's, ain't as many kinds of flowers, but it had the prettiest flowers that looked like birds made of fire. And Mother laughed, and poured her another cold drink. But when the gal went to get up, she heard the woman cluck, "Oh, my dear. Your hair is so tangled. Let me fix it for you."

Her barrettes fall to the floor, and her pigtails come undone. That gal hear the gas on the woman's stove, and see a straightening comb burn red hot, but she don't get up. Mother Bea sing an old, old song and comb through the gal's hair. Burnt hair smell coiled in her nose, washing away toast and sweet blackberry jam. When she done, the gal's hair is bone straight, but she can't remember the name her Mama give her. Mother Bea smile at her, blackberry jam sweet, and call her Sarah. She show her to a bedroom where everything is just her size, and the gal lie on the bed with its yellow bedspread and fall asleep.

Then the old woman go out into her garden and find the flower they call bird-of-paradise. She point at that flower and it sink deep into the dark earth.

NOW

CLEO FINDS HERSELF in what seems to be an endless field of flowers—Michaelmas daisies, Aster's favorite—under a sky the metallic dark pink of expensive lip gloss. No visible light sources. No sun. No moon or stars. No softly glowing streetlamps. But Cleo can see as clearly as if it were noon in summer. There is no wind. In the distance black mountains loom, their peaks snowcapped and glistening in the light from nowhere.

Cleo kneels down to get a closer look at the asters. The ground beneath her knees feels wrong, like soft matting on the floors of fast-food restaurant playgrounds. It doesn't move like soil. The asters feel right. There are variations in the purples, from lilac to indigo. A big, deep plum blossom near Cleo has a thin striation of white on its top petal. But as Cleo looks closer she sees that the variations begin to repeat. A few feet away is another deep plum flower with a white striation; at an irregular place beyond that is another. There has been effort put into disguising the perfection of this field, but it is clear to Cleo that this is a place that has been made, not cultivated, much less one that is wild.

In the chest pocket of her overalls, Cleo keeps a little pouch with important botanicals. She pulls out a little oxblood leather pouch. It contains the powdered root of an *Ipomoea purga* vine. High John de Conquer root. She licks a finger, dips it into the pouch and dabs the root on her tongue. The taste is bitter. She inhales deeply and sings a little song her Gramma-Dear taught her as a little girl. *Rise,* she thinks. She remains solid, on the ground. In the world she has already begun to think of as the wild one rather than the real one, she would have floated upwards like one of Peter Pan's joyous Lost Boys. But whatever was pretending to be gravity in this made world was weighing her down.

The taste of the John de Conquer root still sharp on her tongue, Cleo plucks the big daisy with the white striation. Michaelmas Daisies have the binomial name *Aster amellus.* She plucks the petal with the thin white streak and thinks of her Aster. A memory of being a small girl with tightly braided pigtails, wearing Mary Janes and a hated plaid pinafore, crouching over the sunbaked asphalt at the edge of a church playground, plucking geraniums and letting the petals fly. Like the memory, she says, "She loves me." She blows. The petal is born aloft on her breath and glitters like light on a river. It flies in a straight line towards the black mountains. Cleo follows.

LONG AGO

EVERY DAY THAT woman comb the gal's hair. Every day it combed the gal forget something. But her head stayhard, and her heart still best-loved the garden behind the little yellow house. The woman say call her Mother Bea, but the gal see how she conjure the bees in her big garden with its shut gate, and she call her Other Bee. And she never call herself Sarah in her own head, no matter what the Other Bee call her. She know there are places in her heart where go the people who best-love her, even if they names and faces is combed away. She decide to run away from Other Bee before she combed down to nothing.

She see how the bees bring the old woman they honey, and how every morning she put a spoon of that honey in her tea and drink it. One day, the girl sneak into the pantry and take some honey for herself. It taste like sunlight. It taste like rain. It taste like *conjure.* She smile sweet and fake at Other Bee and ask to play in the garden. Other Bee pat her head and call her Sarah and watch her skip away.

But this time the gal could hear the flowers talk, and she ask them they stories. Hyacinth ain't had nothing but nonsense, and Primrose told lies, but Sister Magnolia told her truths even if she ain't know who the people who best-loved her were. Sister Magnolia come down from her place on the highest tree, and set behind the gal's ear, whispering kindness.

The girl walk among all the flowers, but she never find one that look like a bird on fire and she start to cry. Sister Magnolia ast why she so brokenhearted. And that gal say she looking for a flower that is a bird but also a fire to tell her its story, but she never find it. And the Magnolia whisper she has seen a flower like a firebird from atop the tallest tree.

THEN

I TOLD YOU about magic. We were walking back from a bar downtown and tipsy on the craft cocktails you had ordered for us—last words, sidecars, more than a few french 75s—and I started to talk about how I came from a long line of root workers, and hoodoo priestesses. You turned to me and arched one perfect eyebrow. "You don't believe in all that junk? You don't even read your horoscope."

"Fuck if I sound anything like a Libra," I said. "But magic? It ain't fake."

You laughed again and punched my shoulder. "Come on, Cleo! Magic. I've never even seen an illusionist that convinced me."

Now here was my deepest, darkest places open to you. I think what could have happened if I laughed along with you and changed the subject. If we had ended up on the beach and watched the grunion come in all silvery and slippery. There's a kind of magic in that too.

Instead, I pulled out my John de Conquer root, and I sang my little song, and I showed you I could fly.

And you took my hand, and we danced on air on that dark shore.

NOW

Time feels different here. The light is constant and the shadows do not lengthen as the day passes. The daisies are always at full bloom. In the wild world, Cleo can tell how long she has walked by the ache in her calves, and the pace of her stride, but here movement feels effortless, and except for the ever-nearer black mountains, her path through the field of daisies following the glowing petal might have been a few steps. She wears a watch on her left wrist, a big mechanical brass thing with a scuffed crystal, but it stopped at the time she entered the made world as if she had never wound it at all.

At the base of the black mountains, Cleo can make out a slender spire, silvery in the light. A cascade of water tumbles down from the height behind it. Cleo begins to run, and as if in anticipation of her movement, the guiding petal speeds up. Cleo pushes herself and the field falls into a blur. She feels no fatigue. Her heartbeat is even. Her lungs do not burn in her chest. She rushes along, her feet only touching the ground because the made-gravity insists they must, first antelope fast, then freight train fast. The made world ripples around her like she has cast a stone in a pond. And then she is there.

The spire is the color of alabaster, but with a metallic sheen. It is crowned with an enormous magnolia blossom of what seems to be the same material, all in one piece. *Like The Neverending Story*, thinks Cleo. Leading up to the city is a spiraling, terraced street lined with cypresses and blocky buildings painted blue, gold, cinnabar.

Vines snake down from the flat roofs, and orchids of uncommon size and color festoon the building walls, and bromeliads quiver with dew. Cleo smells the air. There is nothing, not the fragrance of vanilla nor the stink of crown-rot. The glowing petal zips up the spiral street, and she makes her way to the spire.

The terraced street opens out into a broad garden. Cleo sees tulips, daffodils, glory of the snow, birds of paradise, sea holly, and lavender, shaded by ʻōhiʻa trees heavy with bright red blossoms. Plants that favor different climes and different seasons all in blossom, all textbook beautiful. She tastes bile as she remembers the Other Bee's impossibly perfect garden; like a sundew it sparkled and drew her in, waiting to devour her.

Cleo looks up at the enormous magnolia atop the spire. The flower had been a comfort and a balm to her. She had a magnolia blossom tattooed across her back on her twenty-first birthday. When they first made love, Aster kissed that place between her shoulder blades again and again. When Cleo asked why that tattoo and not the clematis on her hip, or the columbine on her thigh, Aster said, "The magnolia's like the pavilion in *The Neverending Story*. You can be my golden-eyed commander of wishes."

Cleo said, "I hope our story doesn't end."

Cleo stands at the base of the spire and puts a hand on its surface. It feels *soft*. Like silk or satin, not a hard, metallic thing. It pulses softly at her touch. Cleo calls lightly, "A-babe?"

Nothing. She presses closer to the spire. It feels warm. She cranes her neck up at the magnolia high above her and shouts. "A-babe! It's me! It's Cleo! Golden-eyed commander!"

The world shudders. The lip gloss sky turns poison apple green and the spire blinks out of existence. The black mountains are now white and textureless. Cleo feels her body under enormous pressure, as if she has been dropped into the deepest part of the sea. An agonizing heartbeat.

Cleo feels that she will be crushed. Then everything rights itself.

Almost. She looks behind her and notices all the sea holly has vanished, leaving gaps in the lush garden. The daffodils look flat, like glossy photographs. The world shudders again and the colors shift, but this time there is no crush and the spire remains solid beneath Cleo's hand. Above her the magnolia blossom opens its petals. Golden light spills out between them. Again, Cleo thinks, *Rise.* This time, she soars.

LONG AGO

THE GAL COME to a place in the garden where the soil is black and the flowers ain't grow."That be where the birds were," the Magnolia say "Maybe they fly away over the wall."

But the gal dig in the soil, and she call out to them. And the bees, them old spies, make theyway to the Mother. Before they get there, the birds-of-paradise spring forth from the earth, and like the gal say, they look like they made of fire. And the gal ask theystory. The birds say they ain't just no flower, but they were in a dance when the world began and so beautiful the hateful moon got jealous. And when they sang about theyfall from heaven Cleo remembered Gramma Augusta playing organ in the church. When they told of they beauty, she remember her sweet mama's eyes, brown but specked through with gold. And she remembered how orange and blue and green the birds in her own great-gramma's garden was, and how that great-gramma call herself Dear.

The Other Bee come with her swarm to stop her, and she call her Sarah, and she beg with sweetness, and she threaten with punishment. But the gal remember her own name, Cleo. And when she spit it at the Other Bee, they both knew ain't nothing could keep her from going back to the yellow house with the garden she best-loved and the people who best-loved her.

Cleo stay hard-headed, but maybe she happy if she ain't find her ending yet.

THEN

YOU CAN LOVE someone so much they are your light and your joy, but the world ain't going to let you just rest with that. The news had been bad; black boys getting shot, queers getting bashed, trans women killed. Some nights we ain't even enjoyed each other's company because something terrible happened. I used to keep track of the names and say them before bed like a litany, but one day it got too many. The world was supposed to be better than this.

You had been out at work since before I knew you, but the last six months someone had sent emails about you. There had been meetings. You told me about a teacher back in England who had committed suicide because they hounded her. There was a night out in West Hollywood when a woman screamed that I didn't belong in the woman's bathroom. Shit, I'm cis.

I don't go online at work. I try to pay attention to the plants and listen to their needs. I didn't know how bad it was until I got home. Splashed all over the internet was a hateful, bullshit article. Trans women are preying on lesbians, the headline screamed. Like you couldn't be both. The article quoted Lita who said nasty shit about "genital mutilation" and how tomboys are made to feel like they're men. It wasn't about you, but it could have been; we both knew Lita, even if I was a tomboy who ain't never once wanted to be a man. I called you right away.

"A-babe? You okay?"

Your voice was brittle. "Guess you logged on."

"Fuck that no 'count Lita. She just mad 'cause no one

wants her Opie-lookin' ass."

You sighed. "Every day there's just another pile of shit. You hear they're introducing a bill in Wyoming to label gender-affirming care as conversion therapy?"

"No. Do they ban conversion therapy there?" I asked.

Another sigh. "Doesn't matter. They don't want us to fucking breathe."

"Do you want me to come over?"

Your voice cracked. "No. Don't you have that big shipment of orchids early tomorrow? Petey will shit the bed without you. And I have a project I'm working on that needs extra attention, so I won't be good company."

"Fuck those orchids. They can survive without me, and if they can't, Petey needs another business. And you don't gotta worry about entertaining me. I'm a big girl. I got books. But I want to be around if you need me." I meant it, and I hope you heard.

"No. I'll be fine. You don't need to come over tonight," you said.

NOW

Cleo crests above the spire. There, in the center of the magnolia blossom, sitting cross-legged among carpels as tall as birch trees, is Aster, clothed in white and holding a crystalline orb the size of a beach ball that she sculpts like clay. Cleo alights next to her. Aster stands. The orb hovers in the air. Already tall in the wild world, she stands a few inches taller here. Her lovely dark skin without blemish or freckle. The mole at the base of her ear is gone. Her waist is thinner and hands smaller. She smiles at Cleo. "You came! But you're early—I still haven't finished everything." She frowns. "I'm having trouble getting scents right. And tastes. It's the difference between grocery store orange juice and freshly squeezed."

"A-babe, I'mma always come for you. But how come you did all this without me?" Cleo feels tears sting her eyes.

"I wanted it all to be a surprise. How did you even get here? I haven't finished the documentation with the instructions."

"I made my own way."

Aster holds out a hand. Cleo takes it. It feels achingly familiar, but there are no scents of onion or pepper. This is the woman she loves, but the woman she loves remains out in the wild world, weakening every moment.

The world shudders again. Colors ripple and warp. Aster touches the orb and stability returns. "There are some glitches I'm working on."

"How long you think been in here for?" Cleo asks.

Aster blinks. "I don't know. A few hours maybe. As long as twelve?"

"A-babe, it's been three days since you told me not to come over. I used the emergency keys."

Aster's brow furrows. "I guess I could put in some sort of internal clock to better track the time." She touches the orb. Numbers glow briefly in the pink sky, then disappear.

Cleo's voice is soft. She squeezes Aster's hand. "In here, you're radiant. Like you used both the butters to moisturize. Your bantu knots is flawless. But out there..." Cleo closes her eyes. "Out there, I think you're dying, A-babe, and I ain't know what I'm supposed to do without you."

Aster sighs and pulls her hand away from Cleo. "In here is a paradise where I—where you and me—can just *be*. Ain't no one to call me a trap. Ain't no dyke this and bulldagger that. Ain't no *niggers*."

"I know. But it ain't real, baby, it ain't *real*. What happens if the power goes out or one of your hard drives fails?"

"The spell should be self-sustaining. And once I'm integrated completely—"

"Spells ain't computer programs. They snakes; they slither away from you and bite when you ain't expect it."

The world shudders again. Cleo feels the crushing pressure. Aster grabs onto the orb and the pressure releases. She looks at Cleo with concern. "I don't know what you want me to do."

Cleo says, "I want you to come home with me."

Aster says, "Home? This is the home I built for us. A home with peaceful gardens for you to work in and anything else we can dream up."

"A garden with flowers that don't smell of nothing."

"I'm working on it." Aster stares at her orb.

"I would do anything for you, you know that. But I can't stay here, and I don't think you can, neither.

"Your world keep tryna shove me out, or maybe it's breaking down 'cause you're breaking down. All of me is here right now, and every time this shit glitch it feel like it's going to crush me out."

Aster looks horrified. "The instabilities have been increasing. But I didn't know they were hurting you."

"Come home with me."

Tears streak down Aster's perfect face. They are pearls with a luster and roundness no oyster could produce. They float up into the sky of the made world. "You said you would do anything for me, and God knows I believe you. And God knows I love you. But you don't know how hard it is Cleo, you just don't."

Cleo shakes her head. "I don't, Aster. But I'm asking you to come anyway." She reaches out a hand.

Aster stares at it for a moment, weeping pearls, and now brilliant-cut canary-yellow diamonds the size of watermelon seeds. As a gemmed cloud forms above their heads, the world shakes. This time the poison apple sky is divided up into cyclopean triangles like a giant geodesic dome. The carpels of the enormous magnolia splinter and fly off in all directions. Cleo feels herself twist and flatten.

A grey chasm opens in the world between her and Aster, who remains perfect and untouched by the tremors. Cleo reaches out towards her, leaning as the chasm pushes them apart.

The grey washes over them. Cleo feels nothing, not warmth, or cold, or pressure. She sees nothing but endless grey. There are no sounds.

Then she feels the warmth of a hand finding hers.

NOW

CLEO FINDS HERSELF on her ass on the hardwood floor in Aster's office. Plaster from the ceiling rains down on her. The window has shattered inwards and broken glass glitters dangerously in the plaster-hazy murk. The server towers are an untidy heap of junk. "Aster?" she croaks.

Aster opens her eyes. She coughs. Cleo crawls across the floor, and over the debris, slicing her knee open on a long shard of glass. She takes Aster in her arms. Aster coughs and breaths in gasps, but her heartbeat is strong. They both weep, collapsing against each other covered in sweat and dust.

Aster sobs. "This is shit. This world is shit. It's shit."

Cleo presses herself against Aster. "I know it is, A-babe. I know. But your woman a gardener, and we gonna grow something from it."

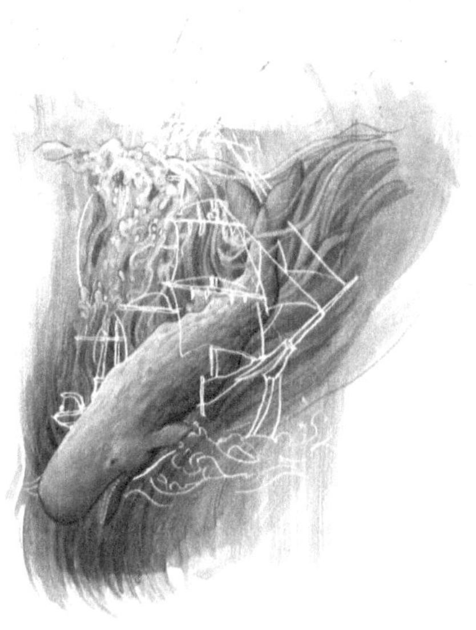

Canst Thou Draw Out the Leviathan

J OHN WOOD BOARDED the *Gracie-Ella* ahead of the crew. He carried his sea chest on his shoulder. In a satchel slung low on his hip were his tools and the three things most precious to him: a lock of his grandmother's hair, a shaving from the first cabinet he had built as a boy, and his freedom papers. No light but the moon, but John could walk the length of the *Gracie-Ella*'s decks eyes closed and barefoot without placing a wrong stop. She was named for the daughters of two men who held her title, and at sea she belonged to the captain, but John reflected that she was his as much as anyone's; his hands had shaped her and healed her, cosseted her and kept her afloat. He ducked down below decks. In the dark he made his way midship to a space he and the cooper shared. The smell of sawdust and resin was a comfort. A few strikes of a flint and the lantern overhanging his workspace was alight. John set about arranging his tools. The work here was sweet. He ran his hand over words he had carved on the underside of the vice-bench. "I hereby manumit & set free John Wood. He may go wheresoever he pleases."

The sixth night out from Nantucket, John woke to find William Harker looming over him in the darkness. John sat bolt upright in his hammock. William put a calloused finger to John's lips. William's voice was silky. "I've been thinking it's been a mighty long time since I've been ashore. Man can develop a thirst."

John groaned, half in anticipated pleasure, half in exhaustion. "Not even a week yet. Ain't your wenching last you a fortnight?"

William bent close to his ear. John could smell salt, armpits, ass. William's breath was hot on his cheek. "T'aint wenches I'm after. I was hoping the ship's carpenter might lend us some wood." William put one big, scarred hand on John's crotch.

John felt himself stir in response. "Captain'll make you kiss his daughter if I'm too ill-rested to swing my hammer come daybreak."

William put his other hand on John's neck. "My harpoon will be all the keener for it, and I can give you practice with your hammer."

John sighed. "Best get on with it. It's summer and the night's nowhere near long enough." He slid out of his hammock and led the big harpooner by the wrist from steerage towards the foretween decks.

John shoved William against the bulkhead and fumbled with his breeches. For all his talk of rest, John was every bit as eager. In the darkness, he traced William's form with deft, curious hands. The body was familiar: the taut belly, the ropey scar high on one hip. He found William's mouth with his own, hungry and biting. They rocked as the ship rocked. John felt the crest of a wave, and in its deep trough heard William cry out. Warm, sticky wetness splashed against his thigh. Slick and sweaty, the two men clung to each other. William whispered, "I'll make you pretty baubles from the bone of the next whale I kill. I'll spend my lay to bring you spices and silks. I'll—"

Light pierced their quiet darkness. John saw the earnestness in William's eyes, before William shoved him away and pulled up his breeches, slipping back the way he came.

John shaded his eyes. Pip, one of the cabin boys, walked past wide-eyed towards the forecastle with a stinking little lantern and a beaten tin cup. If he took any notice of John near naked and smelling of sweat and spunk, no sign of it shown on his dark, intense face. John laced up his breeches and followed after.

"Hoy there, Pip."

The boy spooked. "Hoy, sir."

John laughed. "Ain't no one never called me sir. And you ain't 'bout to start. Name's John, or John Wood if you have to keep formal. Bought my own freedom, and I won't let you give me yours."

The boy gave him an owlish look. "Hoy, John Wood. Never bought my freedom. I suppose I might have stolen it."

John clapped Pip on the back. He pointed with his chin at the tin cup. "What's that, boy?"

"Corn meal." Pip pinched his lips together. "I ain't steal it. Cookie gave it me."

"A nobbin-hearted old skinflint like Cookie gave you near a half cup of it? You must got more charm than I know."

The boy cradled the cup close to his narrow chest. His eyes were wide. "La Sirène knows ways to soften the hearts of men."

John ruffled the boy's hair, as coarse and kinky as his own. "What you doing with that this time of night?"

"Watch."

John watched in the flickering lamplight as the boy wet a finger with his tongue and traced with precision a little boat on the deck. Pip finished his drawing by writing a word strange to John, "*Immamou.*"

John said, "I learnt my letters soon's I got my manumission papers, but what's that word for?"

Pip said, "Protection."

John laughed. "I don't know about that. Ain't no charm against the captain if he catches you sleep on first watch. Get to bed, boy."

Pip blew out the lantern.

Two more days out and early morning John was dumping wood shavings into the cold furnaces of the try works when he heard a foremast hand's thin voice cry from the hoops, "She blows! There she blows! A cachalot!"

The Captain roared, "A sperm whale, aye? Where boy, be quick? She alone?"

"Leeward, Captain! One spray. No more'n a league out!"

"To the boats, boys!" The Captain cracked a rare smile. "Mr. Wood! You keep my ship in order."

John looked among the bodies scrambling over the deck for the other shipkeepers, Cookie, the cooper, the blacksmith, and the steward. He saw they were all awake and above-deck. "Captain sir, all's ready for your return."

The Captain beckoned at the Kanakan harpooner named To'afa—whom everyone called Gospel—with measured speed they headed to the first whaleboat, four crewmen in tow.

William ran to the third whaleboat swinging from its davit. His boatkeeper, the portly second mate, close on the lean, blond harpooner's heels. William looked back at John once and shouted, "I've not forgot me words to you."

The Captain's boat launched first, and the boat with William soon splashed down after.

John heard the Captain cry out, "Take care, you louts, any of you gally this whale and she sounds, I'll stripe you with nine lashes."

Four whaleboats set out leeward after the whale. John stood for a moment at the railing midship watching them row, each boatkeeper urging their crew on faster in low growls. Cookie stood at John's shoulder. He spat a thick gob of phlegm over the side. Cookie sucked at his gums. "Whale brains the night instead of salt horse."

The sun was high when John first heard the crew again. Echoing over the waters, rough voices sang obscenely about the ladies of Cuba before the first of the whaleboats came into view. Towed behind them by the fluke was the carcass of a sperm whale nearly half as long as the *Gracie-Ella* herself.

John yelled for Pip to attend the returning crew. The ship pitched and listed as they lashed the massive beast starboard for the cutting in.

The crew were wet and boisterous, although to John's eyes, tired and the worse for wear. William's whaleboat was the first. The second mate's face was red. "Grog!" He shouted. "Grog for the harpooner!"

Pip ran over with a tin cup full of drink slopping over the edges. William took it from him with both hands and drained it in a single pull. He looked over at John. "That old bull was meaner than my granny, but I keep me promises."

The Captain supported one of his rowers around the shoulder. John ran to help. Ethan, his name was. John knew him to be a serious, quiet boy from Pennsylvania.

His thin, white arm was bent at a ruinous angle. He slumped into John's arms, his face gray. John thought Ethan would have need of his saw. The boy whimpered. John looked to the Captain. "He well?"

"Struck by the blow of a fluke. Plenty of grog and full barrels of parmacety will help him forget, I reckon. Time he comes to collect his lay he'll be smiles again."

John half-carried the boy down into the darkness of the forecastle. He lifted him into his hammock, the boy yelping and shuddering. Ethan's eyes were large and tearful, but John knew he was needed on deck to erect the cutting stage. He stroked the boy's hand. "I'll send the Steward to come look after you."

The sun was low to water when John, stinking and calloused, hammered the last plank of the cutting stage into place. The hands' voices hoarse with hours of filthy shanties—Gospel abstaining. The whale was held fast to the *Gracie-Ella* with great chains. John remembered the injured boy, but knew the Captain would see pulling an able worker away to tend to Ethan as coddling. Every hand was turned to cutting in the whale. The harpooners peeled its skin in spiralling strips known as blankets with long-handled cutting spades. Each blanket piece was so heavy it took John and six others to haul it up. Men already sore and tired with rowing and killing chopped those pieces into smaller sections, to be yet again minced into paper-thin slices known as bible leaves.

William was back in the water with a monkey-rope tied around his waist, passing up buckets full of spermaceti to the two cabin boys, who ran the pearl-colored waxy substance over to barrels, which when full, were hammered shut and sealed under the watch of the cooper. The deck was red and slick with blood. On one of his last passes Pip slipped in the gore and fell on his back. John tossed a horse piece of blubber to the blacksmith and hurried over to the boy. Pip's eyes fluttered shut as milk-fragrant spermacati from his bucket pooled around his narrow frame. John lifted the boy up and staggered against sudden weight; in an instant Pip felt heavier than one of the blanket pieces. He kneeled under the tremendous burden. Pip's eyes snapped open. The boy's expression was hard and made him look far older than his fourteen years. His voice was like thunder. "John Wood. You know me not. But you I know. Your kin called to me for safe passage across my waters."

John groaned struggling to keep the boy upright. "Pip, this ain't sensible. You struck your head."

The boy's look was pitying. "Pip? No. I am the storm and the wind hard behind it. I am the wave and the darkness below. I, the white foam and the shifting sea sand. Do you know me, John Wood?"

John whispered, "Agwe?"

"The blood remembers. Destruction follows your present course. You have until the moon waxes full and wanes again." Pip shut his eyes. John felt the weight vanish from the boy.

The first mate, a tough, wiry man with a parsimonious mouth and thinning sandy hair stood over them. "You niggers pick a fine time for resting. Work to be done, and that spilled parmacety will come out of your lays, so I swear."

Pip squealed. "Sir, t'ain't the Carpenter's fault. Sir? Mr. Wood was just helping me on account I'm so clumsy."

"That so? You'll pay double penalty, then."

John stared hard at the deck so as not to give the First Mate a reason to call him out for insolence. "Sir, now Pip's up and about, if I have your leave, I'm needed elsewhere."

The First Mate scowled. "What are you looking poe-faced for? Back to work!"

That night the fires in the tryworks burned hot. Foul smoke, black as ink, curled up and blotted out the stars. The crew pitched bible leaves into the try pots for rendering.

The cutting in had slowed after the sunset, and John turned his hand to the Captain's whaleboat, which had seen some damage from the flailing whale. It had needed bailing out with a piggin on the way back, but John assessed the boat as being in fine condition, all things considered. He was sanding out a new board to replace one that had been cracked in the hunt, when a shadow distinct from the roiling clouds of smoke fell across him. Without looking up he said, "William, your mama was no glassblower."

William's smile seemed to beam in the lantern-light. He was wrapped in a moth-eaten old bear hide and held out two cups full of grog. "Looks like thirsty work there."

John accepted one of the cups. He took a deep pull, relishing the burn down his throat. He gazed up at William. Shivering cold. Bedraggled. Ridiculous in that bear hide. Reeking of stale blood, salt, and sweat. Beautiful. He said, "You stink. You ain't think to splash some of that ocean water on you whilst you was splashing around with that big fish?"

William smiled and squatted next to John. "That whole time I was fighting that mean old bastard, thinking what you'd say to me when I came back with a mouth full of teeth to carve into something for you kept me going." He rested his hand on John's shoulder.

"Careful. You'll get old Gospel to come over and give's a sermon 'bout the evils of sodomy, and I don't know about you, but I prefer my sinnin' in quiet," John said.

"Be days before a whale this size is barrelled and tucked away, unless the sharks find it first. We won't have any idle hands for the devil's tools, I reckon."

John swatted William's hand off his shoulder. "The devil! You think I'm old scratch?"

"You are a mighty temptation." William's voice turned serious. "That little negro cabin boy? What happened with him? There's been some whispers that he's touched."

"He fell. That's all. Ain't none of you hoodoo-fearing whaler men never fell?"

William pulled John's hand to his mouth and kissed the knuckles. "I just know you're fond of him. I wanted to you to beware if things go sour."

"A great big whale out there in less than a fortnight's time, and you all are muttering about things going sour?" John laughed, but thought of the word "destruction" and all his mirth drained away.

Three days after the cutting in, John was working at the vice-bench, when Ezekiel, the other cabin boy, rushed in, flustered. John looked up from his work. "What is it, boy?"

"Mr. Wood! Mr. Sherman sent me in to find you he said to bring a saw!"

"Bring a saw? where?"

"The fo'c'sle! Ethan Anderson's arm's gone all wrong!"

John nodded, took a moment to select his sharpest and a yard of clean cloth, and followed the boy. The forecastle, never a sweet-smelling place, was rank with the smell of sick and rot. Ethan's twisted arm had turned black. It wept pus through a poultice. Ethan moaned. His face in the lantern-light was pale. His lips were grey. John pressed gently on the arm near the wound and heard a crackling sound like logs splitting in a fire. John pursed his lips. "Zeke, get the boy whiskey."

Ethan's eyes were dull. "Don't mean to gainsay you, Carpenter, but I dreamt of a black dog. Death's coming, and I'd rather go into the sea intact."

"If that arm don't go, death will surely come. You had a misfortune is all. Don't mean the end."

Ethan managed a smile. "My fortune ended the day I signed up to the *Gracie-Ella*."

John looked over to Simon Sherman, the Steward, who stood striped by shadows just beyond the dying boy. He wiped a thin hand across an ungenerous mouth and sniffed.

"Well, Mr. Wood? You heard the man. Leave him to die in peace. Go find Gospel, he'll want to say some prayers for his soul, I imagine."

John put away his saw and found his way to the deck where he saw To'afa looming over the Captain. The harpooner was six and a half feet if he was an inch, and the expression he wore would fit a desert prophet. "Sir, may I have permission to speak plainly?"

The Captain winked at John. He stroked his salt-and-pepper beard. "To'afa, you seem about to burst if I say no. So out with it!"

"Sir, I have served you with the best of my skill. My arm has been yours. Why have you chosen to imperil me with the placement of an unrepentant sinner?"

"Imperil is a strong word." The Captain beckoned to John. "Mr. Wood, what's your perception of sin aboard this ship of mine?"

"Seems to me like pumping the bilge and repairing rotten boards occupies my time in a way that I ain't really considered it, sir."

To'afa wheeled on him. "This is no matter for sly jests. I have seen how you coddle that little heathen. You ought to talk sense to him!"

"Who ain't got sense, now?"

"That cabin boy, Pip. I know you feel a fondness for him out of your shared bondage. But he invokes heathen gods! He makes offerings and worships idols. This cannot stand!"

The Captain stood. Even at his more modest height, he struck an imposing figure. His voice was low and calm. "I trust your objection is to my choosing to have Pip crew my whaleboat? Do you have a suitable replacement for Mr. Anderson? Will you perform the laying on of hands to heal his ruined arm? Or would you prefer I take that half-wit moon-calf Ezekiel to row? I would take the devil himself over that weakling and poltroon. If you have any objections to Pip and his savage worship, I suggest that you live up to your moniker and convert him, Gospel."

To'afa looked thunderstruck. The Captain turned his back on him and walked slow and stately aft.

To'afa looked to John as if he could spit. "Does my faith amuse you, Carpenter?"

John's voice was soft in reply, "It is your faith that has sent me forth. Ethan Anderson is not long for this world. Mr. Sherman has sent me to ask you to say a few prayers for his soul in the next one."

To'afa nodded. "I shall collect my Bible." He looked in the direction of the Captain. "I hope the Old Man does not regret taking no heed of my words on that devil-worshipping boy."

On the day they buried Ethan at sea, one of the foremast hands caught sign of whales. Right whales this time, two, mother and calf. As the crew made muster again for the whaleboats, William pressed something hard and cool into John's hand. It was a sperm whale's tooth, carved into scrimshaw. John recognized his own face carved into the surface, rough edges smoothed away, and surrounded by fanciful flowers. He watched William bound across deck to his whaleboat and smothered a rueful smile.

It was after nautical twilight when the whaleboats returned. The crew sung no work songs, and the slapping of the oars against the ocean struck John as sepulchral. It reminded him of the creaking of a hearse. Once aboard, the Captain's face was pinched and Gospel walked behind him with his head down, muttering prayers beneath his breath. William found John and embraced him in sight of God and the crew. "I'm sorry, I'm so sorry."

John grabbed William by the chin. "What you sorry for?"

"The boy Pip—he…"

"Where is he?"

"The hunt was good at first. Old Gospel got right into her with his whale iron, she were fastened, and—" Tears and snot streamed down William's big honest face. "Whale sounded and snapped two lines. The sea churned into froth. All the whaleboats rocked, mine nearly overturned. Pip. He just dove into the ocean after the whale. It must be a fit of madness. We searched until it was half-dark, but he never surfaced."

"I see," said John in a cold fury. He looked over at To'afa's broad back. "You sure he ain't had any help."

William shook his head. "Gospel's a sanctimonious bastard. But he wouldn't bring no actual harm to a child beyond sermonizing."

"Ain't needed for the cutting in, am I? Reckon I have work to do below-deck," John said.

John was not settled at his vice-bench for more than a moment before William's shadow fell between him and the lamp. Chisel in hand he said, "Thought I told you I had work."

"Thought maybe you could use me in grief as you do in joy." William's tone was bashful.

"You think that? We sailing together on a ship for two years, but after that I ain't so sure I'll sign back on. Seems a short time for you to be studying my grief."

"Six year we sailed together since I was a green hand and you—"

"Bought myself free from a cabinet maker?"

William's voice was patient, pleading. "And you came aboard to be this ship's carpenter, even if you are too skilled by half. What I mean to say is, I don't see no future for me without you in it, John Wood. I keep my lay by, don't spend more than necessary. I've set aside some money. I could set you up a shop to work your trade, buy land for a house and—"

John sighed. "William, I like you. I likes your body. I likes my body when it is with yours. But future? Ain't no future for any negro and a white man in the goddammed Union 'cept as master and slave. I been a slave, I'll be in my grave before I return to that." John looked down at his lathe to avoid the hurt he knew was in William's eyes.

"You're wrong, John Wood. I love you as any man loves his wife. More. I love you so much that it is the filling up and making of me, and sometimes feel like to shatter when you're not near."

John made his expression stony. He crushed down the part of him that wanted to recite to William the Song of Solomon, that wanted to cradle him in his arms and rock him to the rhythm of the boat. "We have sweetness here. Sweetness never lasts. Let it linger on your tongue while it can."

"Do I mean nothing more to you than the cockroach-ridden molasses you sweeten your coffee with?" William clenched his fists.

John looked at the lathe. "What I mean is, we got two years. Ain't no point in expecting more."

"I knew what you meant." William said. John watched him walk away. When William was out of sight, John pulled out the scrimshaw portrait from under his shirt, where it had dangled on a cord to rest next to his heart.

Restless, late to bed, but too tired to find himself elsewhere, John headed midship where he had his hammock. Across from him the blacksmith snored. Above the blacksmith, William slept. His arms hung down limply, and the careworn look on his face had vanished. John put out the lantern. He settled into his hammock, turning to face away from William. His mind raced darkly, but sleep took him in moments.

He dreamt of the poor lost cabin boy Pip sitting at the right hand of a handsome brown-skinned youth with green eyes and wavy hair. The youth rested indolently on a coral throne. His full-lipped mouth pouted prettily, but the sea green eyes were piercing, knowing.

An enormous mirror gauzed over with black crepe rested just beyond the throne. All else was darkness. Pip spoke, but the voice was like the roar of the ocean, and John knew the words belonged to the melancholy youth. "You break bread with thieves. They seek to plunder my seas the same as they have plundered the land before them." He gestured behind him. John knew without seeing that there were hundreds, perhaps thousands of shuffling figures in that unspeakable darkness. The youth nodded. Pip spoke again. "You *feel* them. The whales sing to keep them calm, to prevent them from despairing of never seeing Guinea. These the plundered lost in crossing. I have given them homes and solace."

John felt himself transfixed by those green eyes. Pip spoke in his own voice. "Ain't right what they done to us. Ain't right what they do the whales. They'd burn us both up for lamp oil, and then when we's gone seek to take more."

The dead, John knew they were the dead with certainty, began to shuffle into almost visible ranks beyond the coral throne. They cried out in languages that were strange to him.

The voice of thunder issued from Pip's mouth again. "Until the moon is dark."

John awoke, the visions fresh in his head. He saw that William had already arisen and left his hammock empty. After washing his face with cold seawater, and finding the vision did not fade from memory like most dreams, John resolved to see the Captain.

The Captain had just finished taking breakfast in his cabin with the Mates. The First Mate cast an ugly look at John when he asked if he might have a moment of the Captain's time, but the Captain agreed and bid John to sit at his table. The Mates cleared out in silence. The Captain was still hale at nearly sixty, but John noticed a sag in his shoulders. He looked at John with something like regard and asked, "What troubles you?"

John put his head in his hands. He knew the Captain to be a man of no great faith in things unseen. "Sir? Would you say I am honest?"

The Captain inclined his head. "I know you to be an honest man. And one who never has shirked from toil."

John swallowed. "As I am honest, and for the love I bear you as one who has served under your command for six years… I—"

"Out with it, man."

"Captain, this ship must return to its home port."

"Are you mad? We're less than a month out. We had good fortune with that cachalot bull, but the ship's holds are nearly empty."

By instinct, John fell back into the flowery speech he knew appealed to white men of rank. "Sir, I swear by my life that death and perdition overhang this ship. My only care is to save the *Gracie-Ella* and her crew from this fate. And if I be honest—"

"Enough! I had not thought you to be a fool, John Wood. But if I hear that you have repeated this half-cocked notion of curses and witchcraft to any soul aboard, I swear by my life I'll clap you in irons." He thumped the table with a short-fingered fist. "Am I clear?"

"Yes, sir."

"You may leave."

Another fortnight before the next whale sighting. It was an ugly, overcast afternoon on choppy seas. John was ill-tempered and worse rested. The night before he had troubling dreams of voices calling out to him in the darkness. He and William had scarcely spoken. But he caught William by the arm as the whaleboats swung on their davits. William's face was unreadable. All John managed was, "Take care."

William pulled his arm away. "Take care?"

John felt his cheeks burn hot. "I love you, too."

William grabbed John then, pulled him close to his chest and kissed him hard and deep and slow. Gospel squawked in protest, and John heard noises of disgust, but his heart thundered in his chest loud enough to drown out the roar of the ocean and he kissed William back.

"I'll take care," William said. Then he bounded over to his whaleboat with a joyous whoop.

The moon was a sliver in the sky when the whaleboats returned. John heard the Captain cursing and spouting imprecations across the water. When all the whaleboats were pulled up, John's heart sank. The Second Mate's boat had absent both its boatkeeper and its harpooner. William was nowhere to be seen.

He overheard one of the hands from the boat talking to the steward. "Bad hunt. Lost two. The Second Mate and his harpooner. Harpooner got caught in the line, Second Mate went to cut and got carried over. Whale rammed him up against the boat."

John felt a great shudder of grief. The Captain passed by without meeting his eyes. A choking sound died in his chest, and he ran to the railing and vomited.

To'afa crossed his arms across his chest and surveyed the smashed timber. Without looking John's direction he said, "The wages of sin."

Another hand said, "And after all that loss, damn whale sounded before we could bleed its black heart away."

The next morning a squall came hard out of the west. Waves battered the ship. Its creaks and moans sounded like cracks and wails. Listless but dry-eyed, John made his inspections, filling in leaks with oakum, yelling at Ezekiel to help him pump water out of the bilge. The moon would be dark tonight, he knew. He carried out his tasks diligently with dread growing in his chest like wet rot. He remembered William telling him he saw no future without him and laughed without humor.

That night the storm quieted abruptly. John went above-deck to examine the masts and the yardarm, when in the night's stillness the ocean roiled. Whales in their multitudes flanked the ship aft and starboard. No foremast hand called out this sighting. The Captain himself was left speechless. Right whales, humpbacks, sperm whales, fin whales, in numbers beyond counting were, a phalanx of the sea. Some hand, not clever enough to be terrified, broke the silence to opine that these whales represented riches beyond the dreams of avarice. It began shortly after. A sperm whale rammed the boat with his large square head. There was a crunch and crackle as wood splintered. The ship, over a hundred foot long from stem to stern rocked and shuddered. The Captain screamed, "Mr. Wood! See that you keep us afloat!"

John ran down below-decks and into the hold. The ship shuddered with repeated assaults. A great fracture ran along the keel, and John knew the situation was hopeless. The hold was taking on water fast, and oakum wouldn't slow it down. Still, he picked up his hammer and rolled an empty cask over to the worst leak in an attempt to slow it. Another heavy crash and the ship listed hard to port before righting itself. Thunder pealed. John set to breaking apart the barrels in an effort to shore up the ship. The thunder spoke to him. "John Wood," the voice was Pip's. "You ain't gonna save them, but you can save yourself. You bought your freedom once, and I give it back to you now."

Hearing the truth of this, John reached inside his shirt for the piece of scrimshaw, and clutching it abandoned his task, tearing out of the hold and onto the deck. For a mad moment, John thought to go back, grab his satchel with his grandmother's hair, and his freedom papers, run his hand over the words on the vice bench. Then the whales struck again, and the deck listed, causing John to slide into the mast, where he clung for dear life. There was a scream, and he saw the First Mate tumble overboard into the churning water. The Captain kept his footing, and shouted for whale irons. The last John saw of him, he thrust a harpoon into the air and vowed to the heavens that he would fight and kill every last fish in the ocean.

When the ship righted, John scrambled over splintering wood and dodged falling debris. Crab-walking midship on the port side, he tucked himself into a spare whaleboat, cut it loose from the davit, and trusted fate during the long drop into the night-dark water. A bull sperm whale, black as obsidian but with green eyes, breached nearby, and the force of his splashdown pushed the whaleboat away from the doomed *Gracie-Ella* as she sank out of sight.

He was adrift for two days and a night before a merchant vessel came across him. With kindness and care they rescued him from the leaking whaleboat and brought him aboard their ship, *The Lady Elise*. After he was given fresh water to drink and wrapped in warm blankets, The captain, a young, amiable-looking man with freckles, asked him to tell his story. John did, with some careful omissions. *The Lady Elise*'s captain furrowed his brow. "We picked up another castaway form your ship two nights gone. You must have the devil's own luck."

He saw him then, wrapped in an Indian blanket. Staring up at the star-shattered sky was William.

John fell to the deck. "How can this be?"

William hobbled towards him, his movement slow and aided by a cane. He said, "Leg's seen better days, and I've been pummeled all about like a sack of rotten fruit, but I live." William winced. He dropped the blanket. A red welt the breadth of a thumb was raised around his neck. "Nearly strangled to death and dragged into the sea. But when I was down in the briny cold I heard a voice tell it weren't yet time, that I were given a second chance. Queerest thing, sounded the near exact twin of that poor lost little cabin boy."

John rose to his feet and closed the space between them. When William took his hand, John was still clutching the piece of scrimshaw carved with his image.

Miz Boudreaux's Last Ride

YOU EVER LOVE the pretty right off someone? When I was a kid, had me a BMX, bright red like a candy apple. I rode it all summer long, cresting hills trying to catch the perfect gleam in the sunlight. Only that same sunlight that gave the bike its shine burnt all the sparkle out of it. I forgot about that bike, until three weeks ago when I caught Tommy asleep, nestled in all the pillows with the desert sun falling slantwise on his face through the blinds.

Now, I ain't slept right the night before. My back was sore. My feet swole up like pumpkins. I had an itch just behind my balls. Was a time where I could catch three hours in the flatbed of a moving pick up, or two-and-a-half on some trick's clammy waterbed and feel fresh as ironed boxers the next morning, but them days are gone. So you best believe when Newport–that's our dog– started whining less than an hour after I drifted off, "that goddamn hound" was the nicest thing I had to say about either of them. Tommy ain't stir an inch. So I got my ass up and took Newport out for a walk so he ain't piss all over the kitchen floor. Again. Had to keep Newport on a tight leash, otherwise he'd be liable to chase a jackrabbit into the creosote, or play fetch with a rattlesnake. Weimaraners is hunting dogs, and old as Newport is, he got plenty of sprint left in them long legs.

Come back to find Tommy snoring underneath the window air conditioning unit, my best quilt tucked up to his chin. Still early, but you could already feel the heat coming down over the hills on the wind. Was finna snatch that quilt right off of Tommy when Newport started yapping and growling at the doorway. Wasn't nothing I could see, but Newport's hackles was up and he stood between me and the door like to bite somebody. Last time he was like this, a 'possum had broke through the lattice and got itself stuck between a pier and block in the crawlspace. But he had yapped at the kitchen floor, not an empty doorway. I stroked his flank. "Easy, boy."

Tommy moaned low in the bed behind me, and Newport stopped yapping and slunk off into the kitchen like he was in trouble. Tommy sat up and pulled the quilt tight against his chest. Tommy always got wide-eyed when he was up to no good; just the picture of aw, shucks innocence. But the look on his face now was prim, and half-lidded, like his eyelashes was heavy. Mighta been Tommy's mouth that moved, but it sure wasn't his speech coming out of it. "Davion, cher. You have been keeping yourself very well. I don't suppose I could trouble you to make me a little coffee and scalded milk?"

It was maybe twenty, twenty-one years since I seen *that* look and heard *that* tone, but I gotta say they woulda made an impression even if me and Tommy ain't been over a mountain of associated bullshit. Still, Mama always told me to be polite to a lady, so I took off my snapback and tried my best not to look pissed. "I'd say it was good to see you, but I don't suppose I rightly can, ma'am. Now, Miz Boudreaux, before I bust out the percolator, you want to tell me what you're doing in my husband's body?"

A HALF HOUR later we was sitting at the kitchen table. Me, Tommy's body, and Miz Boudreaux talking out of it. Newport hid behind the sofa, but you could still hear his tail thumping. There was leftover tortillas from the tacos Tommy made the night before, and I whipped up two plates of chilaquiles. Miz Boudreaux in Tommy's body went through three cups of coffee with hot milk, but ain't touched the food. The egg was going cold. She sipped real dainty out of Tommy's best mug. "Coffee is a delight. A shame Thomas has dulled his senses with smoking. Have you ever tried making coffee with chicory?"

"Miz Boudreaux, I'll be happy to make you another cup to go." I took a bite of my breakfast. I should have put a little garlic salt in that salsa. "But you still ain't answered not one question."

Tommy's hands fluttered. His lips pursed. "I have known Thomas a very long time. I was always pleased that he found you, and that you two held onto each other." That heavy-lidded expression ain't do nothing good for Tommy's crow's feet.

"That's sweet, and all, but it ain't Tommy I'm talking to right now, and I need a hand with the chores before the day gets too hot. And again, I don't mean to be rude and all, but is there a point for this voodoo spooky mind control?"

"You have been very patient in indulging an old woman, Davion. It grieves me to cause you distress. I have come here, in fact, to offer you a bargain that may be of great interest."

"Sorry, but can't you just call. Like on the phone? I get that you might not be cool with facetime or skype, but—"

There was a pout that probably would have been charming on a different face. "Alas, Davion, if it were as simple as a phone call, I would not need to make this bargain." Tommy's fingers drummed on the table. "I am no longer among the living, and need someone who is to accomplish a task for me."

I hate this kind of shit. "If your head finna rotate and you plan to vomit coffee on my nice clean floor, tell me now. I can get a bucket."

"Davion! I am not demonic. I am your old friend. We made a bargain before that was mutually profitable, no?"

I sucked my teeth. "Way I remember it, you charged us thirty of the finest portraits of Benjamin Franklin and then said we needed to pony up a collective thirty years of our then young lives in order to get some charms that got us tracked by the goddamn magic police."

"And the charms worked?"

"They worked alright, but we sure didn't use the full time we paid for, and I don't reckon we got a refund on them years."

"A spell costs what it costs."

"Right." Took another bite of my breakfast. Chewed. Swallowed. "Now, I spent twenty years keeping the fuck away from all this hoodoo bullshit because it ain't ever straightforward. 'Mutually profitable' means you want us to do something."

"I left something uncompleted. Something that will not let me rest. If you were to help me accomplish this, I have a prize very much worth your effort."

"I know you're in Tommy. Can he hear this?"

"No. This conversation is between you and me. He is, for the moment, lost. Asleep."

"Why you ain't show up in a ouija board, or talk through the hound? Why put Tommy asleep? You don't trust him to make the right decision?"

"I have never trusted a man."

"I don't want to make no agreements involving Tommy without his say in it."

She stood up in Tommy's body. Walked over to the window. Pulled the curtains closed against the light. "I can smell death in this room. Thomas is a wildfire. Instead of listening to my offer, he would rage and burn until there was nothing left. You, you are a little bit of cool water. I'm afraid the only time for me to broach this with you is now, and it would be difficult for me to return for an answer."

"What's this offer?" I thrust my chin forward, the way I do when I'm itching for a fight.

"I can offer you this: fifteen more years for one of you. One of your lives extended for a decade-and-a-half."

"Why not both?" I asked.

"I can offer it to one."

"Seven and a half for each of us?"

A deep, rattling sigh. "What you ask for is beyond my ability. I have only what I have offered you. Do you accept?"

Shit. My back ain't hurt me that much. I ain't ready to check out, and I reckon Tommy wasn't ready to find religion. "You can't 'spect me to accept without telling me what we got to do in exchange?"

"A long time ago, when I was very young, I came to a place not far from here. I did an unconsidered favor, for a man. I cast a spell that has had consequences. I need this spell undone."

"Don't know if you noticed, but neither me nor Tommy got much in the way of that downhome rootwork shit.

Can't even read a tarot card, me."

"My goddaughter Eulalia will undo the spell. What I need from you boys is protection. She will be physically vulnerable while she does the unbinding, and I need someone to fight for her. A machete would work. No charms needed."

I took a good look at Tommy. A really good look at him. Farmer's tan. Belly big from too many micheladas. Golden hair turned dishwater. Some of the pretty was still there, but he got a mean set to his jaw. I thought about him stealing all the covers, and not getting his ass up to take out the dog I never wanted in the first place. How bad his breath was in the morning. How sometimes I could walk into the front room and find him haunting it like a ghost, with the light from the tv casting colors across his face. I thought the meanest things about him I could.

Then I made my choice.

"SHE CALLED ME a horse?" Tommy shoveled his cold chilaquiles into his mouth. Newport was on the floor by his feet.

"Well, she was possessing you. Guess she could tell how you was hung."

He snorted. Newport gave Tommy's leg a lick. "Be serious, Davion. What happened? What did she want?"

"You still got that .22 Ruger you used for coyotes back when you had the chicken coop?"

"Course I do. In good condition. Part of my inheritance from Uncle Joe, like this house."

"This trailer," I insisted. Newport whined up at me.

"For the last time, it's a mobile home, Davion."

The distinction is still lost on me. We ain't even got a pitched roof. "The gun, Tommy."

"Like I said. Working fine. Plenty of ammo. Ready for varmints. Now what do we need it for?" He tore off some of the white from his egg and slipped it down to Newport.

"Well, the ghost of Miz Boudreaux dropped by with a proposition. We keep her goddaughter Eulalia safe through some bad juju, and we get back the fifteen years we paid her back then."

"Can't say I love the sound of whatever we're keeping that gal safe from, but I don't reckon Miz Boudreaux would risk putting her goddaughter in the way of something she thinks we can't manage." That bad little boy smile spread across Tommy's face. "Both of us get them years back?"

"Both of us," I lied.

Tommy raised an eyebrow. "Maybe death has made that old bat a smidge more generous than I recollect."

I looked down at an envelope with Eulalia's scrawled address on it. "Look like she stay about an hour away. Ain't got no phone number. Hope she's expecting us."

EULALIA'S ADDRESS WAS one of them big ranch style houses they threw up in the late eighties and nineties on loop-de-loop streets with names like Vista Butte Way or Sandstone Arch Circle. Four car garage. Enough bedrooms for your 2.5 kids, plus a formal living room and a den for your home cinema. Looked like someone had laid down sod in the front yard long before the water restrictions had kicked in; most of the topsoil had gone back to the desert. Band-aid colored clapboard. Artificial stonework by the front door. Like a postcard of the American Dream bleached out by the sun. Newport craned his neck to take a gander, then curled up on his blanket in the pickup's flatbed, unimpressed.

A quick check in the rearview mirror to make sure I was still presentable: collar down flat, good sunglasses with the tortoiseshell rims on straight, nothing green in my teeth, and up the flagstone path to the front door, Tommy as my shadow. I pressed the doorbell twice. Nothing for a moment, and my stomach kind of rolled when I considered that Eulalia might not be home. Then a sound of heavy footsteps, and a muffled curse. "Hello!" barked through the closed door.

I smiled at the peephole. Dusted off my 'proper' voice. "Good morning. I hope I have the right address? I'm looking for Ms. Eulalia Jackson."

The door swung in. A big woman near filled the doorframe. I mean amazonian. Taller than Tommy. Muscular, and what my aunties called *thick*. Smooth dark skin, she seemed well acquainted with the cocoa butter. Old school afro with a side-part. Lace-up boots. Camo pants. She looked me up and down. "Knight of Wands and the King of Cups, reversed."

"Excuse me?"

"I think she means us, babe." Tommy said.

The woman nodded. "My tarot reading this morning was all fucked up. Explains a lot. I guess y'all better come in. And no one calls me Eulalia. I go by Jack."

"Nice to meet you, I'm Davion." I shook her hand. Firm grip. "This is Tommy."

"Come on in before I cool the whole Mojave."

The inside of the house was dark and cool. I took off my sunglasses. No lights on and blinds shut against the day. Smelled a little like dust and old cooking. Not unpleasant. Here was somebody who liked they food seasoned. Didn't seem to be a take-your-shoes-off kind of house, but I paused on the tiles in the entryway just in case. Jack beckoned us over to a sunken living room with a rust-colored sectional couch wrapping round two of its walls. She sunk into it, propped her feet up on a coffee table made from a slab of granite. It was covered with papers, maps, and playing cards, including the Knight of Wands and the King of Cups, which was upside down. I sat down. The cushions were soft, but with something springy underneath. Maybe a pull-out bed. Tommy sat on the edge, next to me.

She tamped down tobacco in an old-fashioned pipe. "Y'all hungry? I don't always eat lunch, but I got plenty of leftovers, still good."

I shook my head.

Tommy said, "We already ate before coming out. Thank you."

She chomped on the pipe's stem. Lit it. Sucked in a long drag. Held the pipe in her right hand and blew three perfect smoke rings. "Last night, for the first time since Auntie Melba died, I had me a dream about crawfish. Auntie Melba always used to say if you dream of a trout, somebody having a baby girl, and you dream of a crawfish, there's a boy coming. But for me, all a crawfish dream ever meant was that she wanted me to do something."

Tommy asked, "Your Auntie Melba is Miz Boudreaux?"

Jack nodded. "Great aunt, actually." She chomped down on the pipe again. "Always said I was her favorite. She claimed it was because I was born with a caul, but I think it was just 'cause no one else would get out of their bed at midnight and wait at a crossroads with a cow hoof no questions asked when an old lady in Colorado had a vision."

Tommy nodded. "She was like that. I'm sorry for your loss."

More smoke rings. "She had to be close to a hundred. And you can't say the old girl didn't have a full life. I hope she's at rest now."

I cleared my throat. "I ain't like to be the bearer of bad news, but I s'ppose you could say that's why we're here."

Jack's lips pinched tight. "You here to tell me Auntie Melba's a haint?"

Tommy frowned. "Well she kind of possessed me, which I didn't take very kindly to, to tell the truth."

I gave Jack my we're-all-friends-here smile. "What he means is your sainted Auntie came personally from the beyond to make a request of her—you did say you were her favorite-goddaughter in order to complete a task she left undone during her long, productive lifetime."

Jack squinted. Then burst out laughing. "Can't believe she's been dead for six months and is still finding a way to mind other folks' business. What she want me to do?"

"She said you would be able to undo a spell she cast when she was young. Some place not far from here. Called it Paluma Negro."

Tommy corrected my Spanish. "Paloma Negra."

Smoke rings. "Of course it's that. I've got to go pack my tools. If y'all ain't gassed up your truck, might want to hit a station first. Not many stops where we're going."

WHILE WE WAS waiting outside for Jack, a pair of starlings flitted over and landed on top of a Joshua tree. Newport ain't usually fussed with little birds, but he barked at that tree. The starlings didn't stir, and three more fluttered over to sit next to the pair. Tommy said, "You know they call a flock of starlings a 'murmuration?'"

One of the garage doors in Jack's house lifted. She came out of the garage with an olive drab duffel bag and a bomber jacket slung over one shoulder. Tommy slid into the middle of the bench seat. Jack tossed the duffel in the flatbed, gave Newport a pat on the head, and clambered into the passenger seat. Tommy wasn't never a small boy, even at his leanest, and it was a tighter fit than I'd like.

"Where we off to, boss?" I asked.

"Paloma Negra don't really exist no more." *Click.* The garage door closed. "It was a dying community when Auntie Melba came through seventy years ago. You're going to have to take 200 Street East as far as you can go, and then we're onto some unnamed back country roads."

Tommy said, "That ghost is sending us to a ghost town?"

Jack laughed. "Your man don't say much, but he got some jokes."

"About three." I said. "And he keeps recycling them." I pulled away from the house. We passed three near identical versions on the way onto the road.

"What you know about Paloma Negra?" Jack asked.

Tommy said, "We never heard the name before today."

"Story time, I guess."

Six starlings flew low across the road.

Jack continued, "Y'all know what a sundown town is?"

I nodded. Tommy said, "My dad's from North Platte, in Nebraska. He said my great-grandaddy helped chase all the Black people out of town. Well, Black likely wasn't the word that great-granddaddy used. Bet he'd like to spit to see me with Davion."

Jack said, "Well when you kick everyone brown out of places, they got to end up somewhere. Paloma Negra was a place like that."

Jack's sub-division was a pop of color in the rearview. All too soon it was gone. Ahead was rock, sand, scrub, and Joshua trees. Starlings made a big-ass black cloud across the late morning blue, taking shapes that reminded me of the inkblots the school psychologist shows you.

"Black folk, brown folk, workers from China. They all lived in their little desert town. Back then it was on the shore of a lake. And you'd get big fields of golden poppies blooming in February. Kids'd play in the creek, and someone was always baking something."

"Sounds like heaven," Tommy said.

"I think it was a hardscrabble life. Folk kept goats, and tough little cattle with stringy meat and sour milk. Wasn't near a railroad, so goods was hard to come by and expensive." Jack sighed. "But I think they did okay. Turn left."

I made the turn. The road here was rough, and Newport whined when a pothole woke him from his nap.

Jack said, "But they had a couple of bad years with floods. The creek burst it banks and washed the bridge away. Flash floods from the hills wiped out a whole herd of sheep. And kids drowned."

Another flock of starlings. This time like a choppy wave at sea, then into tight whirlpool spirals. I ain't religious, but I crossed myself. Newport whimpered. I said, "I feel you, dog," under my breath.

"In the third straight year of flooding, the worst yet, one of them kids said he saw a woman walking on the water. Said she had called to him. Called him by his name, and told him to come swim."

"Oh no," said Tommy.

"And when the boy said, 'no,'" Jack's voice sounded strained, "he said the woman on the water had run after him screaming, and pulled at him with cold, wet hands."

Tommy shuddered against me.

"The town decided they were cursed. They pooled their money, and decided they were going to send it down to Mexico to bring in a famous curandera."

More starlings. For a second, the sky was like looking at a film negative of a photographed starry night.

Tommy said, "Was Miz Boudreaux already famous?"

Jack said, "No. Wasn't her. The town had a barber. Joe Woods. Handsome redbone man. Scoundrel. Anyhow he said he had him a new girlfriend, a rootworker from down New Orleans way, a real voodoo queen. And she would do it for half the price."

I can always smell a scammer. "Half the price. So he gon' take most of that as a 'finder's fee'."

Jack said, "All. Auntie Melba was very young, and still fresh to her power. He played on her sympathy and arrogance, and she agreed to do it for free."

Tommy whistled. "Now if that ain't a bitch."

"Auntie Melba came to Paloma Negra with her roots and her powders. With her bone charms, and her scented oils. And she was not ready.b See, the town didn't have a simple haunt she could chase away with loud noises, or trick with an incantation. The flooding was part of the natural way of the land. It seemed bad to the poor folks of the town, but it had always been that way. And it wasn't no malevolent ghost on the water luring kids. The town had an ancient elemental who was tied to the land."

The truck's air conditioning wasn't doing no kind of job keeping up with the noon sun, but I felt cold. Pushed my sunglasses up the bridge of my nose. "What the land need with some kids?"

"Shit." She said it long, like *sheee-it*. "Do I look like a motherfucking elemental entity? I don't know. Maybe that kid made the whole woman on the water up. But whatever the case, Auntie got into a battle with something ancient."

"And she survived?" Tommy asked.

"She survived, and somehow she ended up wrapping that thing up in her magic. She couldn't banish it, but she somehow managed to bind it."

Biggest cloud of starlings yet. Like a thundercloud with beaks. They flew over the pickup, and for a moment it got dark. Newport howled long and high, and the scattered off into different directions, swirling into shapes like smoke.

Tommy said, "So what happened to the town?"

Jack said, "Well it didn't flood no more. But then the creek dried up. And the lake turned into stinking mud before it dried up too. And February came and the poppies didn't."

I said, "And the town died?"

She said, "This whole valley been dying ever since. Make a right."

I turned onto a dirt road. Creosote and Joshua trees edged in, but it was still clear enough for the pickup to navigate through. Through the rear view, I could see starlings trailing behind us like the smoke from an old steam engine.

JOSHUA TREES WAS full of the birds as we got nearer to a cluster of old whitewashed buildings. Bright little eyes was staring out from under spiky branches. It was slow going and bumpy. Newport turned in nervous circles in the truck's flatbed.

Tommy broke the silence. "Any idea where all these birds come from? It ain't mating season."

Jack said, "They're here because of us."

I scratched my nose. "Thought we were here to break the spell."

Jack laughed. "And they sure don't like that! Auntie Melba put certain workings on to keep that from happening."

Tommy said. "So we're protecting you from birds? Like in the movie?"

Jack pointed, "See that church? That's where we're going."

The hills overhead were familiar to me, and I realized we were close to where me and Tommy lived, but on the other side of the promontory. Nestled against the hills at a place where two roads crossed was a small white church. Looked like it was made of mud-brick then painted white, but a very long time ago. Two front windows shuttered over flanked an open doorway. I sparked the truck in front.

Newport barked at the church. Tommy got his gun. Jack got her duffel from the back. As we got neared, we could see little spots of sunlight streaming from holes in the roof, dappling the packed earth floor. A musty stank roiled over as we walked in the doorway, like the church itself had bad breath. At the far end was a stained glass window, wavy but mostly intact. Never paid much attention in Sunday School, but I reckon the picture was the Holy Ghost above John the Baptist Through broken panes, you could see the hills beyond. Black shapes flitted to and fro in the rocks. More starlings.

Newport yowled once, long and sad. Then we heard the sound of wings. The sunlight from above blotted out, and John the Baptist went dark. Jack pulled out a box of kosher salt from her bag. Sprinkled salt in a circle around her. Pulled a little vial of oil from her back pocket and sprinkled three drops on her floor, before tracing a pattern on her forehead. Sat down. She looked at me and Tommy, "What I need y'all to do is kill anything that comes in this space before I finish."

"Anything?" I asked.

Tommy shouldered his rifle.

Jack started chanting. I moved close to the circle and unsheathed my Bowie knife, which I now regretted picking as my protection weapon. Didn't reckon I was faster than a bird, but I hoped I could be a last line of defense. Newport growled.

A high, angry screech rattled the roof. Birds crashed into the stained glass, scattering shards across the floor. Newport loped in wide circles snapping at the windows. I tried to keep still and waited, blade up like a movie samurai. The flapping of thousands of wings sounded like a roar. But through the racket, Jack kept on chanting. Sometimes stopping to trace a symbol in the dirt. There was a loud rush, louder than a subway train, only all beating wings. For a second it went quiet.

Light streamed in from the holes in the busted-up ceiling. Jack continued her chants. I wanted to laugh, but Newport howled again, and then I saw it through the church's open door.

The sky was black and purple with thousands and thousands of birds. They swirled downward in an arc. One time, back when me and Tommy was in Wyoming, we saw a twister far off against the plains. Just come clear out of the skies on a summer day. Well, this was like that, only it was all made of birds screaming.

Tommy said, "here it comes." He planted his feet.

That bird twister wound tighter and tighter around itself until it was the size of a man. Then, the man-shaped cloud of birds took a step and began to walk. Newport ran to the door. He snapped at the bird-cloud and caught a starling. Shook it between his teeth. But the man-cloud kept on with its steady steps. It shuffled over the doorway and I heard the crack of the rifle. Tommy was a good shot. Hit the cloud dead center. For a tick you could see daylight where that flock's heart would be. Feathers burst out in a starburst, and starlings dropped to the floor, but then the hole closed up and the flock took another step. *Crack.* Another dandelion puff of shiny feathers, more birds falling to the floor, but this time it didn't even break stride. *Crack.* This time the head scattered outwards, but like before it continued its path. *Crack.* In the belly. Them birds screamed, but the cloud kept on coming. I knew Tommy was on his last round with no time to reload. *Crack.* In the head again. But it kept coming, and Tommy was out of rounds. The bargain was to keep Jack safe until she finished. So I ran full tilt into that cloud like I could tackle it.

They surrounded me. It was musty, smothering darkness. Tiny feet scratching at my eyes, pulling my naps, wings beating me around the head. Little beaks pecking. Shrieks and squawks and somewhere beyond was Newport's barks. I tried slashing but didn't feel my knife grant any purchase. Something hard hit me in the shoulder. The butt of Tommy's rifle. Slashed again, and this time I hit something. Heard an angry shriek. I bit and I shoved. Felt like I couldn't breathe. And then it stopped. Them birds flew away from me and out the front door.

I sank to my knees. "Babe!" Tommy said, and cradled me in his arms. "Babe, you're bleeding."

Jack said, "It's done. That old heifer made a complicated knot."

The three of us walked outside into the sunshine with Newport at my heel. I reached down to scratch him behind the ear. Maybe that old smelly hound ain't so bad afterall.

The sky went dark again, and I tensed up thinking maybe them damn birds had regrouped for a rematch, but it was just clouds of the ordinary kind. Thunder rolled over the red hills, and we were spattered with rain.

Can I tell you how good it felt? Scuffed up, dusty, ashy, stinking of bird must, and then a clean rain comes and washes that away. We should have gone back to the truck. Jack had already loaded up her bag. But that cool rain washed off all that desert funk, and I saw things different. Tommy's wet hair fell into his eyes, and when he pushed it back, there was a boyish twinkle. The dirt road was already turning into mud, but I ran through it, fucking up my loafers, and I kissed him hard. The way I used to. The way I ain't done for a long time. He smelled clean and new, like green grass.

Newport ran off after something in one of them ruined buildings, and I let go of Tommy's hand to chase after him. Tommy stood in that crossroad before the church. I grabbed Newport by the collar, and that's when I saw it. Water, cascading in rivulets down the hills and over the rocks. It hit the back of that old church in a wave, and put an end to that stained glass window. Roiled around its side. "Tommy!" I shouted, but the stream of it slammed into him and bowled him over.

In that second I ain't think about Miz Boudreaux or his snoring. I didn't think about his medals for swimming. I jumped into the stream after him.

I DON'T KNOW how he found me. But it was Tommy who pulled me out of the water. Tommy whose arms were around me when I bent over double, gasped like a fish and vomited onto the sand. Jack and Newport were quick down the hill after us in the truck, and good thing. As we drove away in the pouring rain, we saw the last of Paloma Negra collapse into a new river.

So I better come clean about my bargain. I asked Miz Boudreaux to give them years to Tommy. I reckon my family is long-lived enough that the death stink she smelt ain't come from me. I'da gave anything to have one more ride on that red bicycle, even after the color had faded. One more time to catch air and feel like I was the king of the world.

It ain't all happiness and kisses in the rain. Tommy still snores too loud, and right now we're holed up in a hotel that smells like mice. See the trailer—I guess I mean mobile home—was on the other side of the promontory, and it got washed away in the storm. We got time and maybe we'll build a home less liable to roam away when you ain't looking. For now, there's just me, and Tommy, and that goddamn hound. But we got each other, and I suppose that's enough.

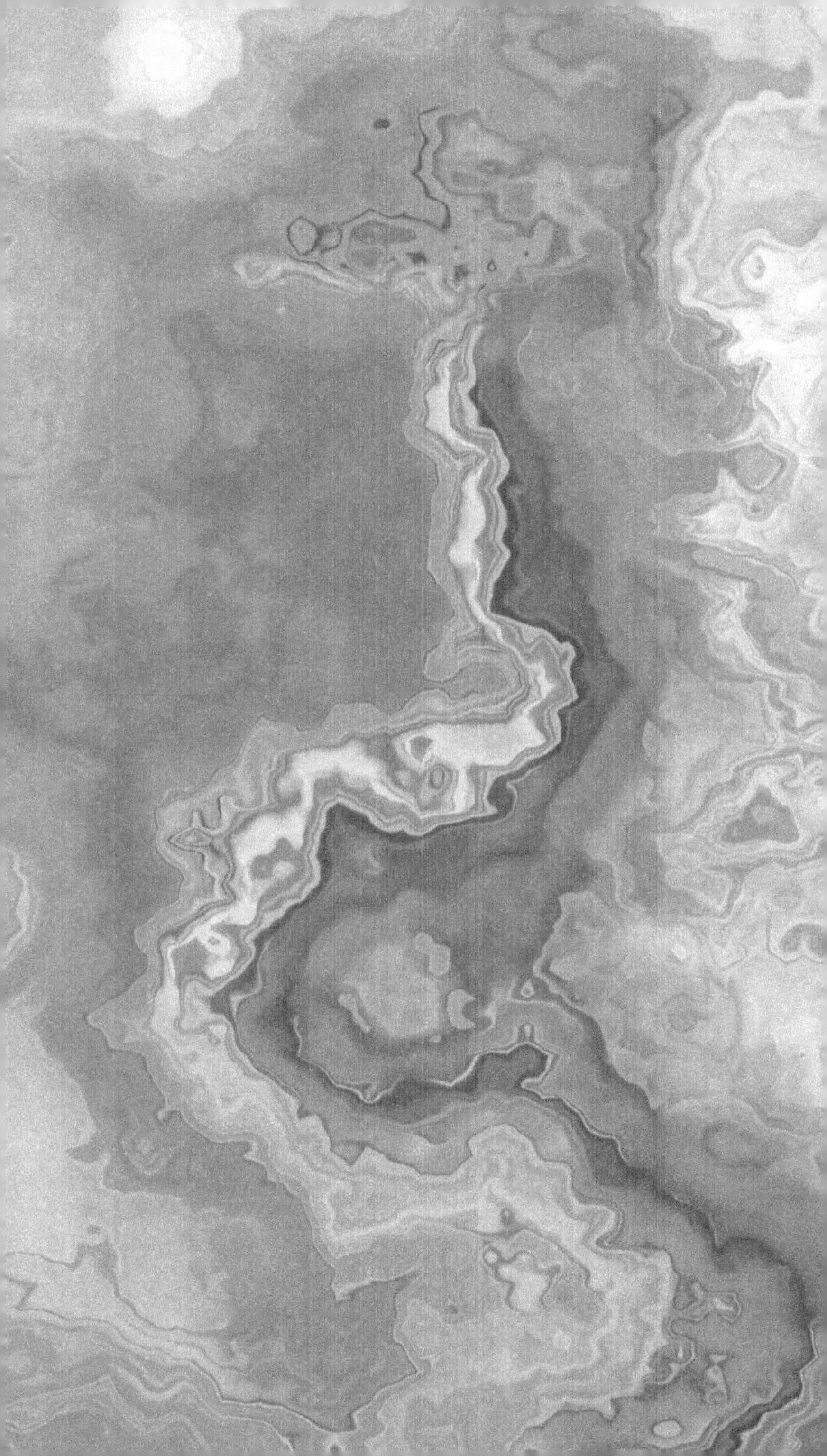

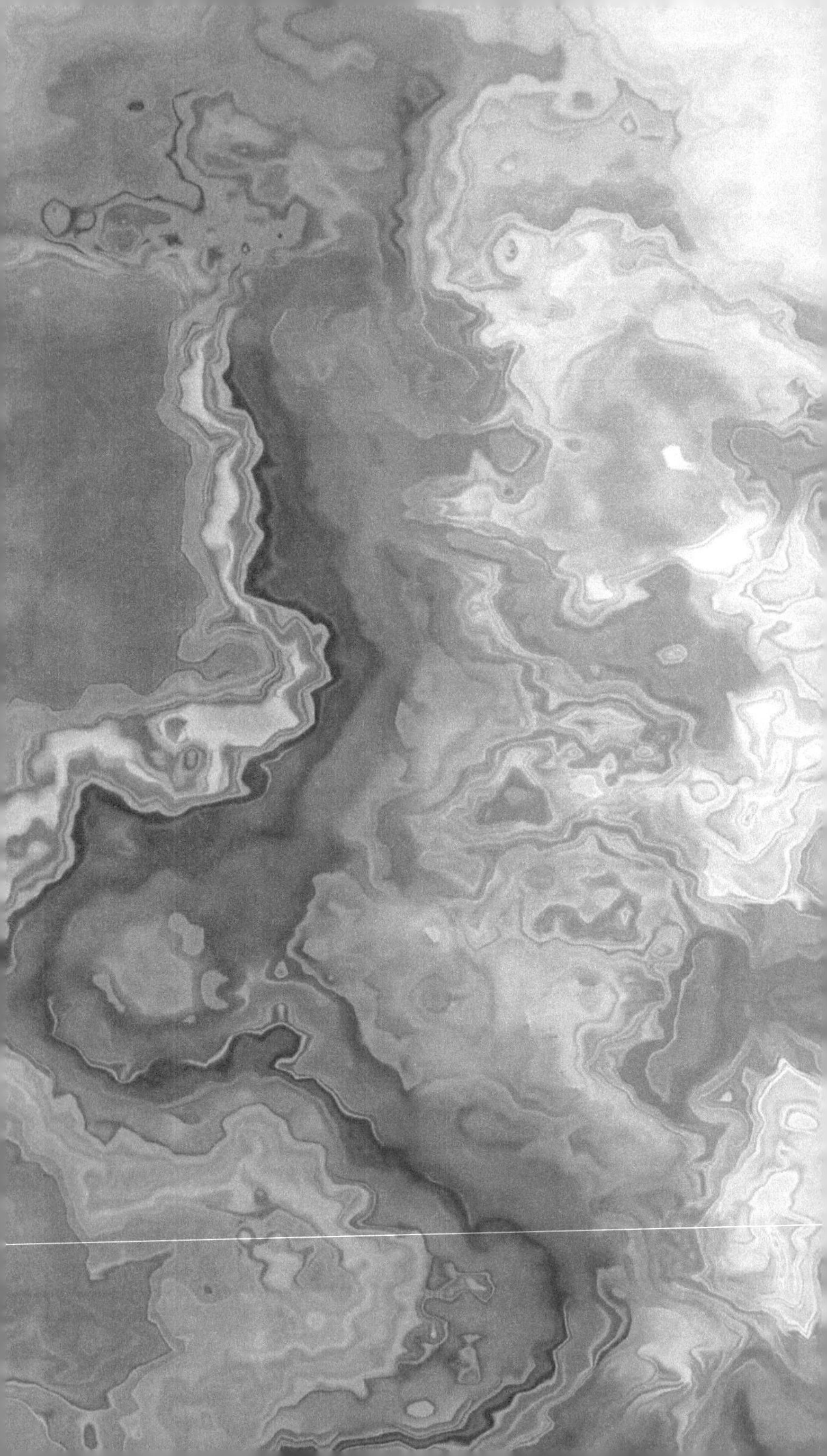

Acknowledgments

THANK YOU TO the editors who believed in and championed the stories in this book: dave ring, Nisi Shawl, Lynne and Michael Damian Thomas, Sheree Renée Thomas, and Troy L. Wiggins

There are so many friends, family, and colleagues who have made writing the stories in this collection possible; who answered questions, who cheered me on and cheered me up, who gave me solid advice that I very well may have ignored, that it would be impossible to list them all. Any faults in the work are my own, many of the graces are due to them. Special thanks to: Mark Baker, Angelique Bell, Jeremy Brown, Angel Camacho, Roz Clarke, Kelley Eskridge, Ruben Ferdinand, Imaad, Devin Johnson, LP Kindred, Tessa Kum, Sam J. Miller, Ian Muneshwar, Dominica Phetteplace, Scottie Roche, Bonita Smith, Ewan Smith, Nalin Taneja, Aaron Uballe, and Eileen Winters.

Story Notes

FEMME AND SUNDANCE

When I was 19, I took a two-day bus trip to see my internet boyfriend in Minnesota.

Two things marked me. We stopped at a truck stop in a tiny town in Nebraska surrounded by dry, dead corn that rustled in the cold autumn wind. The diner had the most openly hostile people I'd ever come across. I had a dollar in my pocket, and felt the stares of every single person in that place. "You don't belong here."

The second is that in the bus station in Des Moines, a pimp sat next to me while I was waiting for the last leg of the bus trip and tried to convince me to come home with him. I sometimes wondered how my life would have been different if I had been more outwardly queer and more combative at that age. That was the genesis of Davion, pugnacious and proud, fuchsia hair and no fucks given.

THE LONESOME SEA

There's a traditional ballad in which a ship's captain promises a hardworking cabin boy riches, and the hand of his daughter, if he will be brave and save the ship from being taken. Once victorious, the captain reneges on his promise, and leaves the cabin boy to drown. I often think about how the cruelty of slavery requires a fair amount of treachery in addition to the brutality of making a human being property.

Even a "good" slave owner is looking after his own interests first. In "Canst Thou Draw out the Leviathan," I wrote that Pip took his freedom. This was how.

BEEKEEPER'S GARDEN

I READ A lot of fairy tales as a child. One of my favorites was Hans Christian Andersen's the Snow Queen. The Woman who knew Magic is presented as a kindly figure who wants to protect Gerda from the perils of her journey. But elements of that chapter always frightened me. Using a comb to erase memories? Awful.

This led to me thinking about how often Black people have pieces of us erased, tamed, and hidden behind Paul Lawrence Dunbar's mask that "grins and lies." That was never going to be a process that Cleo would submit to meekly.

SERVING FISH

THE OLDEST STORY in this collection, and probably the one with the most semi-autobiographical details. Alas, I cannot fascinate a man with my magical gaze, but I did once ride in the back of a U-Haul to a Black gay beach party in Malibu. A statuesque drag queen walking over the sands in Lucite heels is still one of the most magical things I've ever experienced.

This story was inspired by the fairy tale, "The Fisherman and His Wife." But our protagonist is both the fisher and the wife.

IF SALT LOSE ITS SAVOR

I READ AN absolutely horrifying longform article about people working for a defense contractor, clocking in daily, and being proud about their craftsmanship in constructing precision pieces that go on to be assembled as devastating missiles.

These people knew what their work was going to be used for, even if they were never really confronted with the results. But I wanted to explore what would happen if one of the many everyday workers who lend their labor and skill to unwittingly help bring about destruction was suddenly confronted with the notion that even their precarious existence was predicated on the suffering of others. What choices would they make? What would be the consequences?

THE CALCIFIED HEART OF
SAINT IGNACE BATTISTE

EMPIRES CRUMBLE. RELIGIONS lose their faithful. This story takes place in the same world as "If Salt Lose its Savor," although in a very distant locale. The nascent empire that is threatening a proud, ancient city with its crumbling cathedral and grand necropolis is the same one that uses the resources refined in "Salt."

I wrote this story in the hospital, while recovering from a near fatal bout of hypercalcemia. I discovered after this story had been written that Percy Bysshe Shelley's heart had calcified due to tuberculosis, and it did not burn.

DEEP LIKE THE RIVERS

I WAS NEVER a good surfer, but I loved the water. If I had the opportunity to become a mermaid, I would have taken it. It occurred to me too late that "Serving Fish," was really a siren story. I decided to lean into that a little more.

COUNTING HER PETALS

I STARTED THIS story in the hospital as well. I recorded the "long ago" portions on my phone. They felt as if they had to be spoken aloud. That I had to tell them the same way that my grandmothers and great aunts told stories to me.

It's easily the hardest I have ever worked on writing a story. But it genuinely felt like it needed to take this form.

Cleo was always going to grow up to be queer.

CANST THOU DRAW OUT THE LEVIATHAN

I'VE ALWAYS lOVED whales. I used to go on whale watching trips when the Gray Whales made their migration north. Such powerful, beautiful creatures. So gentle! Then I learned about 19 th century whaling, and how Gray

Whales were called "devil fish" because of how hard they would fight when they were hunted. Thinking about how an intelligent, gentle creature can become fierce in its fight to live brought me to a lot of different parallels. And I had hard thoughts about how we, as humans, treat the natural world and our other humans.

The first time I sat down to write this story, John Wood wasn't the viewpoint character. Pip was. But I realized the action had to happen through the eyes of someone not guaranteed divine protection or answers from beyond.

MIZ BOUDREAUX'S LAST RIDE

I ALWAYS WANT to know what happens after our heroes ride off into the sunset. Visiting my mother and aunt in the California high desert gave me an opportunity to find out, in this instance.

It seemed to me that a peaceful domesticity was never really in the cards for Tommy and Davion, and despite neither of them being well-initiated into the world of magic, it was always going to find its way back to them, particularly given the bargain they had made.

About the Author

Christopher Caldwell is a queer, Black American who lives and works in Glasgow, Scotland. He is a recipient of the Octavia E. Butler Memorial Scholarship, and an alumnus of Clarion West. His work has appeared in publications such as *Uncanny Magazine, Apex Magazine, Strange Horizons, and Fiyah Literary Magazine*, as well as the anthologies *New Suns 2, Trouble the Waters*, and *Glitter and Ashes*, among others.

He is fascinated by syncretism, folk songs, and forgotten history. His life's ambition is creating the perfect gumbo.

About the Press

Neon Hemlock is a Washington, DC-based small press publishing speculative fiction, rad zines, and queer chapbooks. Publishers Weekly once called us "the apex of queer speculative fiction publishing" and we're still beaming. Learn more about us at neonhemlock.com and on social medias at @neonhemlock.

www.ingramcontent.com/pod-product-compliance
Lightning Source LLC
Chambersburg PA
CBHW031535310726
48971CB00008B/2490